"What? What am I, Nora?"

She closed her eyes. Having him this close, knowing they were alone once again, was messing with her emotions and her common sense.

"Too much." Her whispered admission landed between them as she opened her eyes and met his once again. "I never should have slept with my boss."

"Despite what you think, we were friends before we were in a working relationship. That night shouldn't have happened, but it did. Now we have to move on."

Move on? Did that include her moving into his house? Did that include him touching her like this? Did that include her fantasies of him bumping up their heat level? Because since he'd unleashed that passionate side all over her, she couldn't help but crave more.

"I'm not sure how we can move on when I'm carrying your child."

* * *

Friends...with Consequences by Jules Bennett is part of the Business and Babies series.

Dear Reader,

Do you love friends to lovers, employee/boss or brother's best friend tropes? Well, *Friends...with Consequences* has all of that and more! Oh, did I mention twin brothers? You're welcome :)

I've had Nora's character in my head for a few years now, but I never quite knew where to put her. After searching Pinterest for character inspo for another book, I found my Zane and everything fell into place from there!

I needed Zane to be pure alpha with a heavy dose of hidden vulnerability. His childhood was less than ideal, so when he's faced with becoming a father himself, he has to really come to terms with all the pain he's ignored for years. Nora is the perfect woman to help him soothe his battered soul. She's wanted him for years, so who better to step in and show him the true meaning of love?

I hope you're ready for this new duet series. If you love this one, Cruz's book is up next with *One Stormy Night*!

Happy reading,

Jules

JULES BENNETT

FRIENDS...WITH CONSEQUENCES

ISBN-13: 978-1-335-58170-9

Recycling programs
for this product may
not exist in your area.

Friends...with Consequences

For questions and comments about the quality of this book, please contact us at CustomerService@Harlequin.com.

Harlequin Enterprises ULC
22 Adelaide St. West, 41st Floor
Toronto, Ontario M5H 4E3, Canada
www.Harlequin.com

Printed in U.S.A.

USA TODAY bestselling author **Jules Bennett** has published over sixty books and never tires of writing happy endings. Writing strong heroines and alpha heroes is Jules's favorite way to spend her workdays. Jules hosts weekly contests on her Facebook fan page and loves chatting with readers on Twitter, Facebook and via email through her website. Stay up-to-date by signing up for her newsletter at julesbennett.com.

Books by Jules Bennett

Harlequin Desire

The Rancher's Heirs

Twin Secrets
Claimed by the Rancher
Taming the Texan
A Texan for Christmas

Angel's Share

When the Lights Go Out...
Second Chance Vows
Snowed In Secrets

Texas Cattleman's Club: Ranchers and Rivals

One Christmas Night

Business and Babies

Friends...with Consequences

Visit the Author Profile page
at Harlequin.com for more titles.

You can also find Jules Bennett on Facebook,
along with other Harlequin Desire authors,
at Facebook.com/HarlequinDesireAuthors!

To my parents, who just celebrated fifty years of marriage. You two are the true meaning of happily-ever-after.

One

Nora splashed cold water on her face, closed her eyes, and willed the nausea to cease. She also willed those power tools to stop, but she'd paid a hefty sum to have her cottage renovated both inside and out. Real Estate in Northern California could get pricey and the market was slim right now, so she opted to revamp her entire place instead of dealing with the headache of a move. And considering the work had only begun, she would simply have to live with the early morning start.

Tearing down walls and expanding the back deck were the least of her worries right now. Two thin blue lines stared back at her and Nora didn't know if this new wave of nausea came from morning sickness or the reality of her unplanned pregnancy.

She pulled in a deep breath in an attempt to get ahold of her chaotic emotions. Falling apart now would not change the fact she was having Zane Westbrook's baby. Of all the people she could have had a one-night stand with...

Zane wore so many hats in her life: her best friend's twin brother, her boss, her friend...and now the father of her child.

Nora needed to get into the office, because she never took a day off, let alone showed up late. But there was no way she could face Zane, and thankfully, his brother Cruz was out of the country on business.

How could she ever look either of them in the eye again? The sickening thought that she'd betrayed her best friend by having a one-night stand with his twin overwhelmed her. Cruz trusted her. They'd been friends for years, well before their working relationship had started.

When the guys launched their lifestyle magazine, *Opulence*, she'd been hired as the social media content director. She took her job and their friendships seriously. Though Zane had always been more standoffish, that never deterred her attraction and desire.

She'd fought for so long.

Except for that one night.

Nora cursed herself for being so naive and vulnerable. She had a weak moment that day, coupled with years of Zane fantasies, and they'd ended up tearing at each other's clothes right there in his office. That had been a month ago and she'd managed to dodge that entire area since.

She grabbed her hand towel and dabbed her face before stepping back into her bedroom. Various clothing options lay draped across the foot of her bed, where she'd set them moments ago…before her life changed forever. Suddenly, wearing her green sweater or her blue wrap-style blouse seemed insignificant in the grand scheme of things.

Nora slid a hand over her still-flat belly and had an instant need to protect her baby. This wasn't quite the way she'd envisioned having a family of her own, but she would do everything she could to make sure her child knew love and stability.

She tightened the belt on her silky robe and crossed to her nightstand. She needed to let Zane know she wouldn't be in today, which was so out of character for her. But she never missed work, so she knew one day wouldn't be an issue.

While she didn't like sending Zane the text stating she wouldn't be in, he was her only option since Cruz was not in the US. Even before their night together, she'd tried to keep her distance or at least make sure they were always in a group with other people. Being alone with Zane had never been a good idea, not with the all of those feelings she'd lived with for years. So she'd tried, she'd really tried to dodge temptation.

But that one moment of weakness had caused her to turn to Zane when he'd offered her comfort the day her beloved Clara had passed. Nora had rescued Clara from the side of the road on a rainy night ten years ago. Clara had been the best roommate and confidant.

Nora had thought working would keep her mind off the passing of her rescue pup, but that hadn't been the case. She'd spent the day sobbing with her office door closed because she didn't want to go home to an empty place.

Then Zane had stayed over late as well, like the true workaholic he was.

Zane always treated her like a business associate, even though he was her boss. The man was too strait-laced and structured with every relationship she'd ever noticed him in. Even if she'd wanted to make a move for him, he'd never given off any vibe that he found her attractive. Maybe he preferred someone taller, with fewer curves, or someone not as loud and outgoing. She wouldn't change who she was, no matter how much she desired a man. Her parents had raised her to be bold, daring, take-charge, and they'd be damn proud of the woman she'd become if they were alive today.

Nora chose not to focus on the negative and sadness in her life. That was no way to live. She'd dealt with many stumbling blocks, but the only way to move forward was to remain positive as much as possible.

After firing off a text to Zane, Nora figured she'd need to go get some hot tea or something else to calm her unrelenting queasiness. The thought of real food nearly sent her right back to the bathroom. Thankfully, the construction crew was outside today, but they would finish up soon and move to the interior.

Was it too early to have the office turned into a nursery?

Nora rubbed her forehead as she padded down the hallway toward the kitchen. She should probably make a doctor's appointment and discuss this life-changing event with Zane before she went choosing paint colors.

A pang of remorse hit her at the fact her own mother wouldn't be here for such a poignant moment in her life. There would be no motherly advice or the bond in helping to choose a name or decorate a nursery. But Nora knew her mother would love this moment and be so excited.

Her cell vibrated in the pocket of her robe and Nora pulled it out to see a reply from Zane.

You're never sick. What's really up?

She stared at the screen, thumb hovering over the keys. How could she reply to that? Not only did she have this secret bomb to drop into his life, she'd also never gotten over their one heated night together. How could she? She'd had dreams of Zane Westbrook for years. Just because his twin, Cruz, might be her very best friend and the brother she never had, and he might even be identical to Zane, never had Nora had brotherly feelings toward Zane. The man had been the star of her wildest dreams since she'd met him.

Cruz had been her absolute best friend and no way would she risk that friendship for a shot at his brother. Not to mention, she absolutely loved her job, so the risks were even higher because her personal and professional lives would be on the line.

Nora had never intended to cross that boundary with Zane. But her emotions had been a jumbled mess and the loss of Clara had crushed her. Still, Nora had insisted on working, but her workday had been a nightmare. By the end, she was an emotional mess.

She should be embarrassed by her actions, but she wasn't. After Zane had wiped her tears away, the only thing she'd felt that night was intense desire. Now that she knew what type of lover Zane was, she only wanted more.

Nora slid her cell back into the pocket of her robe and figured she'd answer Zane later. Right now, she was still trying to wrap her mind around all of the events and combat this nausea. The hammering on her new deck was insistent, but the end result would be worth the headache of living here during renovations.

As she searched her cabinet, she realized she'd forgotten to go to the store for the second week in a row and she had no tea. Now what? She needed to get her queasiness under control so she could do her job. There wasn't a day that went by that she wasn't slammed with work. Which was fine. She loved her job and she loved the mission of the magazine.

She also loved working with the unstoppable duo of Cruz and Zane. She'd thought working for them would get Zane out of her system. Like, maybe he would have been a terrible employer. But the moment she started there, he'd been everything and more. Caring, supportive, strong…sexy. Her desire for him only grew by the day.

Nora grabbed her mug and poured herself some orange juice. Better than nothing, but she didn't know if she had the stomach for the sugar. She padded barefoot toward her home office. Thankfully, this room was on the other side of the house so the construction wasn't nearly as loud, but there would be no escaping the chaos altogether.

As she settled into her plush pink chair behind her brass-and-glass desk, another wave of nausea swept over her. Nora closed her eyes and tried to breathe through it just as her doorbell chimed.

Whoever needed her could check back later. There

was no way she could make it if she tried to move now, not with the way the room seemed to be spinning.

Nora pressed a hand to her stomach and leaned back in her chair. This would pass, she just had to wait it out. She hoped like hell this morning sickness didn't go on for weeks or months like in some pregnancies she'd heard of. If only she hadn't been out of tea, maybe that would have helped.

"Nora."

Her eyes flew open and she jolted upright. The sudden movement caused her stomach to roll even more, and she braced her hands on the edge of her desk to still herself. She focused on the figure across the room and a sudden burst of dread consumed her.

Filling her doorway, looking way too damn sexy, stood the father of her child.

Zane stared through Nora's office space and tried to remember why he thought stopping by unannounced was a good idea. He'd only come here in the past with Cruz when they'd helped her move in and get settled or when she'd had them for dinner a few times. He'd never been alone with her, but her absence at work had worried him. Cruz had always been the nurturing twin, but he wasn't available right now so Zane had decided to step up.

Damn it. He could have called. He *should* have called.

Nora said she was sick, which never happened,

so he only needed to check up on her. Even though he hadn't been alone with her since their night together in his office, he couldn't just ignore her now.

Yet the sight of her feminine curves wrapped in a silky robe and her strawberry blond hair all in disarray only thrust him back to that night. He recalled exactly how amazing she'd looked after their passionate moment in his corner office. He hadn't been able to look at his desk the same way since.

"What are you doing here?" she asked. "And why did you let yourself in?"

Zane stepped into the room, but the pounding from outside jerked his attention toward the windows, where he tried to see out into her yard. He'd completely forgotten she mentioned having some remodeling done on her cottage. How could anyone get work done with that racket going on?

He couldn't imagine what she was getting done. Her place already seemed so over-the-top to him. She had chandeliers in every room, brightly colored walls, and pictures hung everywhere. So. Many. Pictures. The place seemed much too chaotic for him, but Nora had always been extra with everything... which is why she made the perfect social media manager for his magazine.

"I'm here because I'm worried," he informed her. "And, yes, I let myself in. You didn't respond to my message."

He stopped on the other side of her desk and

glanced at the mug full of orange juice, then to her. Her typical pink skin tone seemed a bit pale, which caused another niggle of concern.

"I was on my way into the office anyway," he went on. "And from the looks of things, you really are sick."

He took a second to let his gaze travel over her from head to toe. The briefest of assessments confirmed that Nora looked exhausted and run-down, but he knew better than to voice his opinion out loud. Monday mornings had a reputation for being brutal, but for the first time since he met Nora, she didn't have that bubbly, dynamic personality he'd become accustomed to.

"What's up, and why are you in here working and not in bed?" he added.

Nora curled her delicate fingers around her mug and stared down at its contents. He waited for her to say something, but silence and a thick dose of tension filled the room. Zane fisted his hands at his sides, when he really wanted to circle this desk and lift her into his arms. The need to protect her slammed into him and the foreign concept confused him. The only person he'd ever been protective of was his twin.

Cruz. The heavy ball of dread and guilt Zane carried hadn't lessened any over the past month. He'd crossed the line by sleeping with not only his twin brother's best friend, but also a trusted employee. Any *normal* actions were long gone. He had no clue how the hell to act around her now. Since that night, he'd been a mess, not able to focus and wondering if they'd damaged their own relationship.

Granted, he'd kept her at arm's length for years. He'd had to for his own sanity and out of respect for Cruz. The man truly saw Nora as a sister and always sized up any guy she tried to date. Cruz never thought anyone was good enough for her, which meant Zane had never been able to explore his desire.

Nora let out a little moan and sat back in her seat with her eyes closed, her drink suddenly forgotten. Worry and doubts be damned. He'd merely stopped by to see if she needed anything, and clearly, she needed a keeper because she wasn't taking care of herself.

In an instant, Zane moved around her desk and lifted her into his arms. Her entire body went limp against his as he strode to the plush white sofa across the room. She didn't feel hot like she had a fever, but something had drained her energy and left her weary. She wasn't a drinker, so this definitely wasn't a hangover.

"Tell me what's wrong, Nora."

He was done asking questions and the commotion from outside grated on his nerves and he had no clue how she'd be able to rest with all of that going on. But it was the yawning stretch of silence inside the house that had him growing more and more concerned.

"Do you need to eat something?" he offered.

She shook her head and met his gaze. Those wide doe eyes had always hit him with a punch of lust to his gut. Now was no different...except he'd had her and asking for any type of encore performance was absolutely out of the question. In all their years of working together, he'd been smart in keeping her at an emotional and physical distance. All he could think of now was their intimacy and all the reasons why that had been a mistake.

Cruz had been out of the country for the past month and he had no clue about Zane's night with Nora...he needed to keep things that way. Cruz would be back in a few weeks and Zane didn't want any shift in the way he and Nora interacted.

"I can't eat," she told him. "Just the thought..."

She shook her head again as if she might be sick.

"Why don't you get back in bed," he suggested. "I'll bring your juice and I'll get these workers out of here for the day so you can have some peace and quiet."

"No."

She pressed a hand to his chest and Zane had to grit his teeth and will himself to think of anything else other than the way her curves fit so perfectly against him. He couldn't help her if his mind kept going back to that night, when she'd been so upset and he'd only tried to comfort her. But years of pent-up tension and desire had overwhelmed both of them.

Zane carefully placed her on the couch and stood

over her, hands on his hips with worry and confusion consuming him.

"You can't work," he commanded. "You can barely hold your head up. I'll take you to the doctor."

"No."

She scrambled to her feet, clutching her robe when the material parted between her full breasts. When she started to sway, Zane jumped up and gripped her arms.

"You're going to the doctor," he demanded. "Let's get you dressed."

When he started to pick her up once again to get her to her bedroom to change clothes, she held up her hands.

"Wait, just calm down." She pulled in a shaky breath and continued to clutch her robe. "I don't need a doctor. I mean, I do, but not because I'm sick. I—I'm pregnant."

Zane stilled as the room seemed to close in on him.

He misunderstood. He *had* to have misunderstood. But the way she stared at him, with her chin tipped and tears gathering in her eyes, he knew he'd heard correctly and Nora wasn't messing around.

"You're the father, if that's what you were going to ask next," she added.

He honestly didn't know what he was going to ask next because he was still wrapping his mind around the first part.

Zane raked a hand over the back of his neck. "We were careful."

Nora let out a humorless laugh and went back to the sofa. She eased herself down and rested her head on the high arm.

"Not careful enough," she murmured, closing her eyes.

Damn it. Here he wanted answers and instead of helping, he'd opted to grill her when she clearly couldn't even hold her head up. What a jerk.

Fear gripped him at this life-altering news, and he couldn't even imagine how she felt. While he'd never wanted a family, and was quite content being in a committed relationship with his company, he'd heard enough from Nora to know that she did want a family someday...and likely not from her boss.

Zane lifted her into his arms once again, but this time, he headed out into the hallway. He'd been here enough to know the layout and knew which room was hers. Even with keeping a safe distance since they'd met, he did know quite a bit about Nora. If not from her own mouth, then from his brother, who typically spent all of his spare time with her.

Zane had known for a long time that Nora didn't have family of her own and his...well, he had Cruz and that's all that mattered right now. But what would Nora do for support? She only had her work family and her very close relationship with Cruz.

That meant Zane would have to step up and be

that man in her life, but there was only so much he could do. She and the child deserved so much better than he could offer them. Oh, monetarily they'd be set for life, but if she wanted any type of emotional bond or connection, there was no way in hell he could be that man.

"You don't have to keep carrying me," she murmured against his shoulder. "I've got morning sickness, that's all."

He didn't like seeing her this way, and he sure as hell didn't like feeling helpless. There was nothing he could do as the control over this situation slipped from his grasp. He prided himself on staying on top of things, making sure his life ran in the neat and tidy order he'd created.

Obviously, no matter how well planned or detailed his world was, he'd let years of need override common sense. Now their night together, which should've always remained a secret and in the past, would be forever out in the open and part of their future.

"I can't go back to bed."

Her words pulled him from his thoughts as he moved through her open living area and down the other hallway leading to her main bedroom. He'd never stepped foot in her room before, but he imagined it was just as bright and feminine as the rest of her home. No doubt she had photos hung all over in there as well, including several selfies with her and her dog. The woman clearly loved pictures.

"You aren't going anywhere else," he informed her as he turned the corner. "And I'll be here in case you need anything."

"Zane—"

He spun around, sliding a finger over her lips. "Not up for debate."

Nora's eyes widened for a fraction of a second, holding him in place. At this point in the quick evolution of their relationship, he truly didn't know who had seduced whom. Maybe touching her now hadn't been his smartest move, but he wouldn't keep arguing this topic.

Without a word, Zane dropped his hand and continued back in the direction he'd been going.

The pounding from the construction crew grew even louder as he got to this part of her house and Zane gritted his teeth. Trying to get any peace here would be virtually impossible. And for someone who already felt bad, someone who was pregnant and needed even more relaxation than normal, this situation was not ideal.

He set Nora down on the edge of her bed and propped his hands on his hips. "There is no way you can rest or work or even think straight with all of that racket going on."

She offered a soft smile, one he'd seen so many times over the years. It was her smile that had pulled him in from the start. She had the sweetest little dimple to the right of her full lips, and he had a really difficult time not staring at that mouth and remembering all the places she'd touched him.

His body stirred and he cursed himself for being vulnerable enough for someone to matter. That right there was why he'd been stony his whole life, why he'd gotten the reputation for being hardened and tough. He couldn't afford to be any other way. He refused to be hurt, and he refused to turn into a heartless man like his father, who'd abandoned everything and everyone around him.

"I hadn't planned on being here while they were working," she retorted. "I would normally be in the office at this time. But my morning sickness won't last forever."

"How long does this last?" he asked, realizing he knew absolutely nothing about pregnancies or children.

Nora shrugged. "From everything I know with friends or books I've read, everyone is different. This could last days or weeks or even the entire pregnancy. And even though it's called morning sickness, it can happen anytime during the day."

Being sick for months sounded like a nightmare. Not to mention months in a home being renovated inside and out. Zane rubbed his palm along his bearded jawline, trying to figure out the best solution. Nora and the baby's health was the most important aspect right now, so their needs had to take priority.

"You'll move in with me."

Nora jerked and her shocked expression paralleled his internal nerves. He hadn't thought about what he wanted to say, the words simply came out. He'd never asked a woman to live with him, never wanted a family at all...not after the hell he grew up with. But this moment was unlike any other he'd ever experienced, which meant he had to think differently than ever before. He also had to care for what was his and not be a deadbeat like his own father.

"I'm not living with you," she countered with a snort. "We're having a baby, not playing house."

Nora's strength and drive had always been one of the things he admired about her most. But he didn't want to get into a verbal sparring match over this. He had to make her see that this was the best solution for the time being. If she moved in with him until he could figure out what the hell to do, then maybe he would have a better grasp on suitable next steps.

No matter what, Zane would be a hands-on dad. He would have his child in his home. Maybe he'd never wanted fatherhood, but here it was, and his child would never, ever lack for stability and protection.

But first, he had to get Nora on his side.

"You're sick," he started. "You've got construction crews surrounding your house, and soon they'll be inside. This is temporary until we can figure everything out."

"I can stay at a hotel."

Damn, she was stubborn. Any other time he'd find that quality sexy, but not when it was directed toward him.

"What would we tell Cruz anyway?" she added. "He's going to hate us."

Guilt gnawed at his gut, but there was no erasing history or escaping the future. While they'd been able to hide their intimacy for weeks, soon that wouldn't be possible.

"He won't hate us." Zane hoped. "But we need to worry about you right now, so get dressed and let's get you moved into my place."

When she only glared at him and didn't volley back an excuse, he took the moment as a win. He had no clue what the hell he'd won, though, because his twin would feel betrayed and Zane was about to have the family that he never wanted.

Two

The only good part about this day was that her nausea had ceased. Maybe if she hadn't felt like death earlier she would have been able to argue her point with Zane back at her place. As things were now, though, she found herself in a lavish spare room on the second story of his palatial estate. Her entire living space could fit into this bedroom, and that didn't even count the adjoining bath.

The drab place really needed some things on the walls. To start with, an updated paint color would go a long way.

"That's the last of it."

She turned as Zane stepped through the doorway

carrying her final suitcase. She stared at her matching luggage and nearly laughed. She couldn't even recall what all she'd thrown in there. She'd been so annoyed at Zane for pushing, at herself for caving, and had just started tossing things inside. She did remember the books, though. Reading had always been her outlet in life, and now more than ever, she needed an escape from reality.

"Thanks. Go head on into work," she told him. "I'm fine."

He crossed his arms over his broad chest and leveled her gaze. The intensity of his stare always had a tingling effect on her. How could he hold so much power over her emotions? And that was before the pregnancy. Now? Well, now they were bound for life.

How ironic that the one man she wanted more than anything, the man who was off-limits, would now be an integral part of her life forever? This wasn't how she wanted him or how she wanted to start her own family. Her entire world had just shifted into something completely unrecognizable.

"What?" she asked when he continued to stare.

"You think I can just go into work now like we have nothing to discuss?"

She didn't want to discuss anything. She wanted to just pretend this was normal and not face her emotions, because if she did, she had a very real concern she'd break. And that could never be an option.

Zane emanated strength and power. The man

prided himself on control, and she respected and admired him for it. He possessed qualities that made her strive for perfection in her own life. He had an intensity that she couldn't help but be drawn toward.

"Fine," she conceded. "Let's discuss where we can hang some pictures if I'm going to be staying in here. It's rather stark and boring."

Zane's unwavering glare had her shrugging. "What? I'm serious," she added.

"I'm not redecorating and there's nothing about our styles that is the same. Can we focus on the actual issue?"

"I'd rather just get to work," she replied. "I'm not feeling too chatty."

"We have to talk about this, Nora. Everything has changed and we can't pretend it didn't."

Maybe they couldn't, but for now, she needed to focus on the one constant in her life. "Our lives haven't stopped and neither should our work."

Nora crossed the room and grabbed the handle of one suitcase to wheel it away. Before she could turn, Zane's hand covered hers. The jolt she'd always felt before had intensified since their night together. She hadn't even thought it possible to have stronger feelings toward Zane, but her body clearly hadn't gotten that message.

She brought her attention to his and that penetrating stare had her heart skipping. This was absolutely not the time for her heart to become involved. She had enough of a mess on her hands.

Zane had always been the standoffish brother, the quiet, mysterious one. He and Cruz might look identical, but their personalities were on opposite ends of the spectrum.

"Stop avoiding me." He slid his hand up her arm, his fingers curled inside her elbow. "You've avoided me since that night and now you're forced to talk about it."

She pulled away because having his touch right now, or anytime, was a bad idea. She'd taken part in enough bad ideas lately. Now she had to keep her head on straight to figure out how to fix things.

"We don't need to talk about that night," she told him. "We need to move forward and figure out how we're going to deal with Cruz, because I cannot lose his friendship, too."

"Too?" Zane stepped around the luggage and towered over her. "You think you lost my friendship?"

Nora closed her eyes and tried to gather her thoughts. She couldn't concentrate with his piercing gaze on her and that familiar, woodsy cologne surrounding her. And when he got this close, in her personal space, he made her feel so small and delicate. She'd never been labeled as small by society's warped standards, but she'd also never been ashamed of who she was. And Zane had seemed to appreciate each curve. He'd cherished her in ways she'd never experienced with a lover. His hands, his mouth, his body—a night with Zane had far exceeded any fantasy she'd ever had. The way he...

No. She could not keep thinking of that night.

"You're the one who's been dodging me since then," he continued. "You haven't stepped foot into my office and you only want to communicate via text. So who do you think lost a friend?"

There was no mistaking the conviction in his tone. Clearly, she'd tried to push their intimacy to the back of her mind, and in the process, she'd pushed him away as well.

"Is that what we were?" she asked. "Friends? You always avoid me if Cruz isn't around, and when you are around, you're..."

"What? What am I, Nora?"

She closed her eyes. Having him this close, knowing they were alone once again, messed with her emotions and her common sense.

"Too much." Her whispered admission landed between them as she opened her eyes and met his once again. "I never should have slept with my boss."

Zane's thumb stroked the inside of her elbow. "Despite what you think, we were friends before we were in a working relationship. That night shouldn't have happened, but it did. Now we have to move on."

Move on? Did that include her moving into his house? Did that include him touching her like this? Did that include her fantasies of him getting hotter?

Because, since he'd unleashed that passionate side all over her, she couldn't help but crave more. Zane's touch kept rolling through her mind, and working or having any type of rational thought had been rather difficult this past month.

"I'm not sure how we can move on when I'm carrying your child."

Zane's lips thinned as he released her. "We need to set some rules."

Of course he'd want to set rules. Zane was the master at rule following…except that one night when he wasn't. Zane had a plan for everything and always played by the book in both his personal and business worlds. That's one way he and Cruz differed. Cruz was more of a laid-back, carefree guy. Perhaps that's why he and Nora clicked so perfectly as best friends. She typically didn't get flustered at life and tried to enjoy the ride…but she wasn't so sure about this ride. The unknowns and worries of starting her family when she wasn't ready terrified her; not to mention the lack of her own mother in her life to learn from and seek advice.

And then there was the fear she had of telling Cruz the truth.

"That night can't happen again."

Zane's words pulled her from her thoughts. As much as that night shouldn't happen, that still didn't stop her from desiring that very thing. She'd wanted his touch for years. She'd wanted to know how Zane was as a lover. Now that she knew, could she ignore how beautiful and memorable everything had been? For that one night, that one *moment*, her whole world had been absolutely perfect.

"I'll talk to Cruz when he gets back," Zane added. "This isn't something he should hear over the phone, and that will give me a bit to figure out what to say."

"What is there to say?" she countered. "We had sex, I'm pregnant, now we're living together. Even I can't wrap my mind around this pace we're going."

"We're not living together," he corrected, rubbing his hand down his stubbled jawline. "This is temporary, so you can avoid that construction and I can help when you're not feeling well."

"And how exactly is that going to work?" she asked. "You can't stay home all the time and neither can I."

Zane let out a bark of laughter. "I own the company. I assure you, we both can stay here and work if that's what is needed."

There was no way she could stay in this house with him twenty-four hours a day. Hell no. Being here at all set off all sorts of alarm bells, but he did have a point about all the construction and her being sick and needing to rest more. She just hated that he was right and this was her only option.

"I'm not shirking my career." Nora reached for her suitcase once again and wheeled it over to the bed.

"I take my job seriously and I'll be going into the office. I just might have to come in late sometimes."

When she started to lift the luggage, Zane was across the room in a flash, hoisting it up onto the bed. She turned and stared, hands on her hips.

"Are you going to keep hovering?" she asked.

"Yes."

"Then I'm moving back to my place."

A corner of Zane's mouth kicked up. "You'd rather live in that mess than let me help?"

She had to set her own rules and boundaries as he'd mentioned. Her sanity couldn't handle trying to deal with a pregnancy, sickness, and living with the only man she'd ever wanted.

"I'm only staying here because it is the smartest choice for now," she explained. "But I don't need you doing everything for me and I don't need you acting like my big brother."

Zane's dark eyes narrowed, his nostrils flared. Clearly, she'd struck a nerve. Good. He'd been striking her nerves for years.

"I assure you, I don't think of you as my sister," he growled, then took a step back. "I'll let you get settled in, but I'm working from home today. I'll be in the office if you need me."

He turned and left, then shut the door behind him. Nora let out a sigh she hadn't even realized she'd been holding. Nothing had been resolved in their little chat, but what could they say at this point?

She still wanted him. Pregnancy or not, her feelings hadn't changed. Clearly, he thought they'd made a mistake, which actually hurt. For years she'd kept her emotions in reserve, afraid of what would happen if she exposed her truth. Granted, sex could all just be physical and superficial, but not to her. Not with him. Yes, she'd been in a vulnerable position that night, but she'd also known what she was doing.

Nora unzipped her suitcase and wondered just how living with Zane would go, because she couldn't imagine how much self-control she'd have to have to sleep under the same roof as him and ignore that invisible tug of desire.

Zane stared at the layouts for the summer covers. Normally, he approved everything his design department sent his way, but right now, he hated each and every image. Nothing felt right and he had no damn clue how to fix things.

Like the woman in one of his guest rooms.

What now? They hadn't worked through anything other than the fact that she would stay here and she didn't want him hovering. Well, too damn bad. She was pregnant with his child, and despite what she wanted, he would be present in every single aspect of her life from here on out. If she'd gotten pregnant by someone else, he'd still worry about her being so sick, but this was *his* child.

The idea of her carrying another man's child sent

a ball of rage bounding through him. He didn't want her to be with anyone else. He didn't care for that mental image of another man touching her sweet curves or driving her to the brink of passion.

But he couldn't have her, not again. There was too much at risk—their friendship, their working relationship, the solid connection between her and Cruz, and his own bond with his twin. So, here he was, at a stalemate with himself.

He couldn't even fathom how Cruz would react. Oh, Zane had a pretty good idea, considering Cruz had always been territorial with Nora. He would feel as if they'd snuck around, as if they betrayed him, when that was the furthest thing from the truth. Cruz would be upset at first, but he would come around. Zane just hoped that once he did come around, there would be no animosity between any of them.

Thankfully, Cruz was still out of town on business, so that would give Zane time to think. None of this was ideal and he took full blame. He'd hidden his attraction to Nora for too damn long. He'd taken advantage of her when she'd been most vulnerable and now he had to be strong for her. No doubt she was scared, and he knew enough about her childhood and the loss to know her situation hadn't been ideal—something solid they had in common. She'd lost her parents as a teen and Zane had pretty much been raising himself then as well.

Oh, his father had tried reaching out over the past

couple years, but his sins couldn't be erased quite so easily and Zane wasn't feeling too forgiving.

One problem at a time.

Zane refocused on the layouts before him on his screen. Business he could control, and that's what he needed right now. All of this outside of *Opulence* would have to be dealt with carefully, so he had to get his head on straight and get his footing back under him. He also had to figure out how to enter into a co-parenting agreement with Nora and pretend that he still didn't want the hell out of her.

Their evening had been too rushed, too frantic. He wanted to take his time with her and explore each and every curve of her body. He wanted to look into her eyes as she came undone, knowing full well he was pleasuring her.

His cell vibrated on his desk and he glanced down to see his brother's name. Zane stilled, not really in the mood to chat, but he had to act like everything was fine or Cruz would know something was up.

Sometimes this twin intuition could be a curse.

Zane swiped the screen and put the call on Speaker.

"Hey, how's Costa Rica?"

"I left there yesterday," Cruz stated. "I'm in Puerto Rico for the next couple days, remember?"

Zane rubbed his forehead. "Yeah. It's been a morning. I just forgot."

"What's wrong?"

Of course Cruz would pick up on something in the first five seconds of their call. Zane expected no less.

He shifted in his seat and eased back. "Nothing I can't handle. So, did you find those new models for our fall shoot?"

Even though it was still early in the year, there were still so many things to get done for each installment. They had to line up the fall models and start working on the holiday soon as well.

"A couple with potential," Cruz confirmed. "I'll send you the specs. I actually came across another social media account that I'm thinking about returning to. I'll send you her information as well. Her name is Mila and she's currently in Miami."

Zane and Cruz might be the CEOs of *Opulence*, but they still were very hands-on in every process of the magazine. They'd started out strictly online, more out of boredom than anything. They'd been working on getting back into ranching, something their father had stolen from them, but they'd needed income in the process. They'd tapped into low-key social media accounts to find models, products, and journalists. One thing snowballed into another and their magazine had taken off. The fact they found their talent and related content from "no name" faces online was a huge hit and something that hadn't been done before.

Twelve years later, that's still how they did business. If someone from *Opulence* reached out, you'd

better believe you were about to catapult to super-
star status.

"Did you see the piece that Annie in marketing
wants us to consider for the wedding season?" Cruz
asked. "I know we will be cutting it close, but I don't
see why we can't pull it off."

"I did. I'll get to that shortly."

"I actually think that would be good for Nora,"
Cruz added. "She's got an eye for special occasions,
and weddings just seem like her, don't you think?
And she's going to hate this, but she'd be the perfect
model, too. And that's how we'll save time, because
she's already in-house."

Something stirred in his gut, something he couldn't
quite put a label on. Instantly, the image of Nora in
a wedding dress hit him. She'd made no secret about
the fact that she wanted a family someday. She had
stars in her eyes and would make anyone a great wife.

Not him, but someone.

"Zane?"

His brother pulled Zane back. "Yes, she would
be great. I'll make sure she gets the information and
mention modeling, but you know she hates attention."

"She's stunning and vibrant," Cruz countered.
"All she has to do is put on a dress and be herself."

Zane didn't want to think of her as a bride, so he
circled back to business. "When can we expect you

back in the office? Or are you just going to keep traveling and meeting beautiful people?"

Cruz laughed. "Hey, you had the opportunity to do this instead."

True. Originally Zane was going to be the one go meet with their prospects, but he'd traveled so much recently, he told Cruz to go ahead. Perhaps if Zane had gone, he wouldn't be in the predicament he was in now staring down the new role of fatherhood.

Would Cruz have crossed the line with Nora when she'd had such a tough day? Would he have taken that friendship to another level?

Another burst of jealousy hit him. No way in hell would he want Cruz with Nora. He shouldn't be so damn territorial, but he couldn't help how he felt. Cruz always said she was the sister they never had, but never had Zane considered her family. Not once. She was…well, Nora. She was part of their inner circle…and now they were truly bound for life.

Zane had every bit of confidence his brother never had any type of sexual feelings toward Nora. Zane never would have made a move if that were the case. But there would still be a hurdle to overcome and an uncomfortable talk to have.

Movement in his doorway caught Zane's eye. *Nora. Of course she would choose this moment to show up.* He jerked upright in his seat and held up a hand to prevent her from speaking. Nora froze and remained in place.

"Cruz, someone just stepped into my office. Make sure you send me all the specs on the new talent and I'll take a look at the other project, too."

"Sounds good."

Zane disconnected the call. "What's wrong?"

"Did you tell him?" she asked.

"No. I'm not going to yet."

Nora pursed her lips and crossed her arms around her midsection. "This doesn't feel right, lying to him like this. He'd never do that to me."

Zane came to his feet and rested his hands on his hips. "He likely wouldn't, but I'm asking you to just let me handle this when he gets back."

When she continued to hold his stare, Zane moved around his desk and figured he better distract her before she got too wrapped up in her thoughts. The best way to handle this was in person. Without a doubt.

"Did you need something?" he asked her. "You're looking better than this morning."

"I feel better." Nora pulled her hair up into some twisty knot on her head and used the rubber band from her wrist to secure it. "I was going to get something to eat, but felt really silly invading your kitchen."

Zane laughed. "Nora, you've been here before. This is no different."

Her head tipped, and in that instant, he flashed to the night in his office when he'd dropped to his knees to remove her heels. Now she stared down with that same tilt, the same heavy-lidded stare…which only meant one thing.

She still wanted him.

"Everything about this is different," she fired back. "I don't know what the protocol is."

The protocol would be for him to keep his distance and treat her like the friend and employee she'd been for years. There was no other option. Getting involved in a personal relationship would only lead to a complete disaster. That family unit was everything she wanted, but it wasn't the life he wanted. There could be no middle ground, and he would never purposely hurt her. Leading her on, making her think there was anything between them, would only be a jerk move.

Zane crossed the office. The closer he got to Nora, the wider her eyes got. Everything about their relationship had shifted. He'd tried so damn hard to keep her in that employee box, to respect her relationship with Cruz. In an instant, years of self-control and willpower had vanished.

He stood within inches of her now. Her mouth parted, her gaze dropped to his mouth. Zane gritted his teeth and clenched his fists at his sides. She still wanted him. Oh, she'd fight it because she didn't want to make things more complicated, but the obvious facts stared him in the face. He had to get a grasp on this situation before things got worse.

"There's no protocol."

He wanted desperately to reach for her, wanted to know if that skin still felt just as silky as he recalled. He wanted to lean in and inhale that sexy scent along her neck. If he rested his hands on that dip in her waist and tugged her close, would she respond as boldly as she had a few weeks ago?

Damn it. One of them had to remain in control. A baby had been thrown into the mix, and they had enough issues on their hands without getting swept up in hormones, lust, and memories.

"You have to stop looking at me like that."

Her attention snapped from his mouth up to his eyes. "Like what?"

Zane propped his hands on his hips and sighed. "You're not naive, Nora."

"No, I'm not," she agreed with a defiant tip of her chin. "But you can't tell me you don't think of that night."

Every touch, every kiss, every single pleasurable moment played over and over in his head like a damn movie. Getting Nora out of his mind would be nearly impossible, but he had to try. Their intimacy might have been unplanned, their night rushed and frantic, but she'd left an impression so deep in his soul...

"It doesn't matter," he countered, needing her to believe what he said. "What matters is getting our friendship back on track, focusing on this child, and talking to my brother. Nothing else can come into play unless we're talking business."

"You think you can live under the same roof as me and not want to see if that night was just a one-time thing or if there's more?"

Oh, she was trying him. Good thing he'd shored up an exorbitant amount of strength and resilience in his younger days because this woman was going to test every last ounce of both.

"I don't think I can. I know it."

Three

Nora truly wished Zane would have just gone into the office. She dodged him after she grabbed something to eat earlier. If she stayed in her room, maybe he would do his work and leave her to do hers. At least she had a large antique desk in the corner of her space, and with the balcony doors open, she also had some much needed fresh air. With a little stretch of the imagination, she could pretend she was on a vacation.

A vacation with a man she wanted to strip down but was totally off limits.

Earlier, she hadn't meant to mention anything about the other night, but every time she looked at him, that's all she saw. His passion, his energy…his hard, well-toned body. How could she ignore the persistent stirrings inside her?

Nora closed her laptop and figured she might as well grab a book and head out onto her own balcony. Reading always relaxed her. She could escape her own problems and focus on someone else's for a while.

She'd at least thought to grab a few novels from her pile at home. Although she didn't pack enough bras and underwear, she still figured she had her priorities in order. Besides, she could do laundry here.

As she went to her bedside table to choose a book, her cell vibrated in the pocket of her cardigan. With her demanding schedule and workload, she always had her phone within reach.

The second she saw the screen, she cringed. There was no reason to be afraid to answer Cruz's call. He didn't know anything and he was her best friend. If she didn't answer, he'd know something was wrong.

She understood Zane's standpoint that they shouldn't say anything until Cruz was home, but, on the other hand, they were lying to the one man they loved more than anything. Cruz trusted them and she'd been more loyal to him than anyone in her entire life.

With a deep breath, Nora pasted a smile on her face because she knew he'd be able to read her mood in her tone.

"Hey, what's up?"

"I thought for sure I would have heard from you after Zane filled you in on the wedding spread," Cruz told her.

Nora hadn't heard of any such thing, although Zane's mind might not be too focused on work today. She didn't want to throw him under the bus, but she'd definitely discuss the shoot with him after she got off the phone.

"We've been a little busy," she replied, which was not a lie. "Aren't you doing your own thing? Why are you checking in on me anyway?" She dropped her voice to a teasing tone. "I knew you'd miss me being gone this long."

Cruz's laughter filtered through the line. "I actually miss the way you'd grab my favorite mocha on the way into the office, so I guess I miss you."

"You only use me for my coffee runs—I get it." Nora picked up a book and started toward the balcony. "So, how many lovely ladies do you have dinner plans with?"

"It's like you think I find someone each time I travel."

"Don't you?"

She stepped onto the balcony and glanced around at the adorable seating arrangement. A nice sectional surrounded a small fire pit, and off to the other side was a bistro table for two. She had no idea where Zane got these pieces, but Nora highly approved. Maybe she could get the name of the store or website and shop there for her own renovations…and the nursery.

"Nora?"

"What? Sorry," she replied. "I zoned out for a minute."

"Is everything okay?" he asked.

Nora settled into the corner of the sectional and curled her feet to the side. "Nothing I can't handle."

"That's exactly what Zane said to me earlier." Cruz sighed. "Are you two keeping something from me?"

Nora stilled, gripping her phone even tighter. "Why would we do that?"

"I don't know, but if something is going on at the office that I need to know about, just say it."

The office? Nope. Everything was perfectly fine there. The rest of their world? Not so much.

"The office is fine," she assured him, thankful she could at least tell the truth about something. "Just enjoy your trip and find our next superstars."

"Will do, but ping me and let me know what you think about the wedding idea. I can't believe he got you to agree to model."

Model? She hadn't agreed to anything and had no clue what Cruz even referred to. Were they out of their minds? She wasn't a model, far from it.

Before Nora could ask what the hell he meant by that, Cruz had disconnected the call.

Why didn't Zane come to her and explain this idea? Did he want to try to control her work now?

He'd already admitted he would hover, but now he was going too far in volunteering her to model and then not even cluing her in on the big project. She absolutely would not stand for any of this.

If Zane wanted to lay some ground rules, they could start with him not acting like a Neanderthal.

Nora modeling? The whole idea was both laughable and terrifying.

She set her cell and her book to the side and walked back through her room and into the hallway. She had no clue where he'd be, and his house was ridiculously large. Both Cruz and Zane had homes that rivaled a small hotel, yet both men lived alone. She never could make sense of that logic.

Nora went down the hallway and glanced into the rooms. She had no idea which one was his, but she didn't see him anywhere. She wrapped her cardigan tighter around her waist, wondering why he liked his house so cold. Who else was he expecting? Penguins? She should have packed her fuzzy socks and slippers.

When she reached the first floor, she checked his office only to find it empty as well. Then she stopped. The faintest noise had her moving toward the back of the house. He had to be in the home gym. The clanging of weights seemed to echo as she got closer, and the moment she stepped into the double doorway, she froze at the most glorious sight. How could she not stare at such beauty?

Zane wore nothing but a pair of tennis shoes, gym shorts, and a healthy sheen of sweat. The man had muscles everywhere. Who knew calves could be sexy?

Desire spiraled through her, but before she could make a quick exit with this image seared in her mind, his eyes came up to meet hers in the wall of mirrors.

Busted.

Zane kept his attention on Nora in the doorway. He didn't turn around, didn't need to. Her eyes were huge, her mouth agape, and she looked like she was trying to decide between tackling him or running away.

He always used weights and fitness as an outlet for frustration. If anything warranted an escape, this day had to rank at the top of the list.

"I didn't mean to interrupt," she told him.

Yet, she didn't make any move to leave. Zane set the weights back on the metal frame and turned to face her. He propped his hands on his hips and wondered what had prompted her to seek him out.

Though hc wasn't sorry. The way her eyes raked over him only turned him on even more. The dead last thing they needed was heightened sexual awareness. Yet here they were.

"Something wrong?" he asked.

"Yes. Two things, actually."

Wonderful. At this point, what did another issue

or two matter? Hopefully, this could be narrowed down to work and he'd have an easy solution.

"Let's have it," he told her.

"Why are you purposely keeping work from me?"

Confused, Zane reached for his bottle of water on the bench. He twisted the cap and took a long drink, trying to process her accusation.

"I'm not keeping anything from you," he replied, screwing the cap back on.

Nora crossed her arms and shifted her stance. Clearly something or someone had set her off, but her anger needed to be redirected. All he'd been doing was trying to figure out how he could be a father, when the notion had never been on his list of goals. Mainly, he'd been having a staff meeting with himself about not getting involved with employees... which had never been a problem until now. He'd let his desire override common sense, but never again.

He'd done so well keeping Nora in that friend/employee zone for so long. He had to circle back and make sure she stayed right where she belonged.

"Then why didn't you tell me Cruz had an idea for me to start planning and working on? And that you wanted me to model for some wedding project?"

Her accusation pulled him from his own thoughts. Just because his personal life imploded, didn't mean his business could.

"Cruz had the idea of you modeling," he countered. "I talked to Cruz this morning, as you know.

Then we got distracted and I had other calls and emails. I'm not keeping anything from you."

Though he wouldn't hesitate to pull back if he thought she was stressing herself or not taking enough breaks. While he knew absolutely nothing about pregnancies, he knew that Nora looked like hell this morning. He had to take care of her even before he took care of his business, which would be quite different from how he ran his day-to-day life. He'd made a commitment long ago to his company, vowing to never have a family after the mess he grew up with.

"I'm not model material."

"Why not?" he asked. "You're striking and curvy, and that's the look we want with this wedding piece."

Did he need to point out the obvious? Nora had a beauty unlike any he'd ever seen. He couldn't imagine a man alive not finding her desirable.

"I never want in front of the camera unless it's for a regular picture." She slid her hands into the pockets of her oversize cardigan. "We have too many beauties available, and those we haven't used yet, for you all to be looking my way. I'm the social media girl, which means I'm behind the scenes."

"Maybe we want you *in* the scene this time," he offered. "There's a time crunch for this project and you're here. I can have everyone come here for the shoot—we'll make it in the afternoon, when you are feeling well."

Nora sighed and stepped into the gym. "It's not the modeling nonsense that had me irritated. Cruz is going to know something is up if I act like I don't know what's going on with my own job. So when he threw that idea at me, I had no idea what he was talking about. I hate lying to him."

She dropped her arms at her sides and let out another frustrated breath. She glanced around the workout room before moving around. Zane recognized her nervous energy and he kept his eyes on her as she seemed to be contemplating her next move. Tension continued to curl inside him and he absolutely loathed that feeling. In all the years he'd known Nora, the only tension he'd had was that of want and need, desire and passion. Now that they'd crossed the proverbial line from their stable working relationship, he didn't know if they'd ever get their footing back under them.

"We should call and tell him what happened." Nora rested her arm on the treadmill and stared across the room. "The longer we put this off, the angrier he will be."

Zane nodded in agreement. There was no doubt Cruz would be upset, but that's why the news couldn't be delivered over the phone.

"He'll be angry no matter what, but let me deal with that," Zane told her. "I know him better than anyone."

"We should both tell him," she countered. "We're a team now, Zane. Whether you like that term or not."

Oh, he didn't. The only team he wanted to be on was one that made *Opulence* larger than the day before. It was the only way to stay alive in this industry, and that meant continually rebranding, reinventing, and recalculating everything you'd done in the past.

If he faced the fact that he and Nora were a team, then he'd have to enter into something deeper with her than he was ready for. He had no clue how this whole co-parenting thing worked, but surely, there was a website or a book or something that would tell him.

Nora nodded toward the weights. "Do you do this every day?"

"Yes."

Her eyes came back to his bare chest and Zane found all his thoughts running together. There were too many emotions, too many red flags waving all around.

"I told you not to look at me like that," he warned.

Nora laughed. "Then put a shirt on. You have everything on display—where else should I look?"

"Anywhere else."

She propped her hands on her hips and raised one perfectly arched brow. "You're saying if I stood here with no shirt, you'd look somewhere else? Unless, of course, you like your women on the smaller side."

Zane found himself crossing to her in two strides.

He curled his fingers around her arms and leaned over her until her head tipped back and she had nothing else to focus on but him.

"I don't have a size preference, and I think I made it clear in my office that you are both sexy as hell and desirable. You make me forget every bit of common sense and the outside world, so don't ever doubt your power with this gorgeous body. You'd bring any man to his knees."

"Zane."

When she whispered his name like that, he had an even more difficult time trying to keep his head in the right space. She'd panted his name when he'd lifted her onto his desk and, again, when she'd come undone all around him. Nora was the most passionate lover he'd ever had and the only woman he couldn't get out of his system.

"I can't maintain my control when you look at me like that night." He softened his tone, trying to keep his composure. "You make me remember."

She reached up and slid her thumb along his bottom lip. "You do the same to me."

Everything about her made him want to ignore the alarm bells and ignore the fact they were sneaking behind his brother's back. He wanted to forget she was one of his top employees, but she carried their child now and his role had drastically shifted.

"This can't happen," he murmured.

"It already happened."

Just one taste. Maybe if he leaned in a bit more

and grazed his lips across hers, he'd know if his recollection was off or if they were that good together.

Nora continued to hold his gaze, pulling him in even deeper. Zane inched closer and when her eyes dipped to his mouth, he couldn't take another second without her touch.

He covered her lips with his own, opening her to recapture the full experience. Nora swept her tongue against his as she wrapped her arms around his neck. Her body pressed fully against his, from shoulder to thigh. Her hips aligned perfectly with his…just like he recalled.

He gripped her hips and held her right where he wanted as he let weeks' worth of passion consume him and this moment. He'd wanted his mouth on her since that night. He'd dreamed of getting these sweet curves back beneath his touch.

Just another minute and he'd release her. He just needed more.

A chime echoed in the room and pulled Zane from his thoughts and the heated moment. He took a step back, trying to pull in a full breath. But Nora still stared at him, a hunger in her eyes that matched his own.

The ringing echoed once again and he turned to the weight bench where he'd set his phone. And the name on the screen killed the moment, because his father was the dead-last person he wanted to talk to right now.

Four

"That's not going to happen and Cruz is out of town anyway."

Nora stood in the hallway just outside the gym, trying to catch her breath from their heated exchange and not eavesdrop on his personal call. But she was human and couldn't help herself.

"No, Barrett."

Barrett. Zane and Cruz's father. Zane never called the man Dad and had made it clear he wanted no relationship with him. Cruz, on the other hand, had been coming around over the past year or so. Nora knew enough about their past to know the boys' mother had passed when they were around ten. They'd lived on a sprawling ranch and had every intention of taking over when they got older, but after their mom died, their father had given up on life. Nora didn't know all of the details, but the family lost the ranch, thus taking the boys' future and life away. Cruz had opened up to her a couple of times about his past, but she'd seen the pain when he spoke, so she never brought up the topic.

Clearly, Zane had never forgiven his father, but Zane had a harder shell to crack than Cruz. The guys were completely different, yet their identical appearance could be confusing for some. Many of the employees at *Opulence* still couldn't tell them apart, but Nora never had a problem—the way her body reacted to one of them had always been a dead giveaway.

Cruz always seemed like a big brother and best friend all rolled into one. They'd formed a connection instantly stronger than most siblings had.

Then there was Zane. Not only were Nora's feelings for him far from sisterly, she didn't think of him as a best friend, either. If she did, she would feel comfortable telling him all of her secrets and sharing details about her personal life. If Cruz hadn't tied them together, she doubted that he would have ever glanced her way or given her the time of day. With the way he always seemed to keep her in that employee, low-key friend box, she was just as surprised as anyone to be carrying his child.

"You lost that right years ago."

Zane's low voice pulled her back to the moment.

She shouldn't still be standing here listening to a conversation that had nothing to do with her. Zane always valued his privacy, something she could appreciate.

A string of curses echoed out from the gym and Nora battled whether she should check on him or leave him be. She didn't know how this was supposed to work with her living here. Were they just to pretend everything was normal? Were they supposed to act like that kiss never happened?

Nora closed her eyes and rested her head against the wall. If Zane's cell hadn't interrupted them, she wondered where they'd be now. Would he have stopped or would he have continued to pleasure her like he had the night at his office? Did he actually find her desirable or did he simply find her convenient?

There were too many questions, too many unknowns. And where did her sudden insecurities come from? She'd never worried what a man thought of her before. Never cared if he found her sexy or perfect enough. She wasn't ashamed of who she was or how she looked. There weren't many people who could say they loved their bodies and were proud of their accomplishments, but Nora learned long ago that confidence carried so much weight for someone's self-esteem.

Yet Zane had managed to crack her steely surface

and she wondered if he actually found her attractive or if she was just another—

"Nora."

Her eyes flew open and Zane stood mere inches away. She hadn't heard him step from the gym, but that gaze of his hadn't diminished. The intensity beneath those heavy lids struck her core and heated her all over again. How could just one stare be so potent? How could she see him on a completely different level than his twin when they looked exactly the same?

Because Cruz was a friend and Zane… Zane commanded her attention without saying a word.

"I didn't mean to listen to your conversation." She straightened from the wall and pulled in a breath. "I just needed a minute. I'll let you get back to your workout."

Just as she started to turn, Zane curled his fingers around her elbow and tugged her closer. Nora held her breath as she met those dark eyes.

"This can't keep happening," he all but growled.

"You mean when you kissed me?"

"There were two people in that room," he countered. "But if we're going to figure out this parenting situation, we can't keep getting distracted."

Nora tipped her chin up. "Is that what I am to you, Zane? A distraction?"

His lips thinned as he inched even closer. The need to reach for him, to see if they could pick up where they'd left off moments ago, was too strong. But she didn't know if he had no interest in her or if he'd waged an inner war with himself. Zane held his emotions and thoughts too close to his chest and she couldn't penetrate that tough exterior.

Maybe he didn't let anyone in. Perhaps he had his reasons for being alone and standoffish, but for one night, they'd both been vulnerable to each other. She'd never seen him console anyone or offer her a shoulder to cry on. She'd never had a one-night stand before, let alone with her boss and friend. She wasn't quite sure of the protocol here, but moving in with the man seemed like another wrong move. Yet here she stood, with a plethora of emotions and nowhere to put them.

"You distract the hell out of me," he admitted through gritted teeth. "Working together, now a baby, and you living here is..."

He shook his head and muttered a curse.

"You told me to come here," she fired back. "I can go back to my place or get a hotel during the renovations."

His eyes snapped back to her. "No."

That one-word command sent conflicting feelings spinning through her.

"You can't have it both ways, Zane. I realize people don't deny you anything, but you can't kiss me like that and then get upset about the fact I'm here. This was all your idea."

The way he stood there just staring really ticked

her off. How dare he get upset over a kiss they clearly both wanted.

"I'm only here until my renovations are done," she went on. "I'm not here for games, and despite how much I still want you, I won't put myself in that position again."

She jerked her arm from his grasp, hating that she'd just admitted her need. She couldn't undo her words, though, so now she'd just have to deal with it.

"Get back to your workout, Zane."

She moved down the hall and turned the corner, finally pulling in a deep breath once she'd gotten out of his line of sight. He wouldn't follow her; he had too much pride for that – just like she had too much pride to stand around and argue feelings and who kissed whom. All she knew was she couldn't trust her emotions right now. Between the upheaval that used to be her calm life and the unexpected pregnancy, she needed to decompress and take a moment to herself.

Nora headed up to her room and closed the door. A nice bubble bath with one of her books would put her in a better mood. But what would she do about the fact that her lips still tingled and her body still ached? She had no clue what the remedy was, but if she didn't keep her distance, she had a feeling the next kiss would lead to something more.

There weren't enough curse words to fit his mood. Between having his father interrupt the hottest kiss with the woman of his every waking fantasy and then having her throw that kiss back in his face, Zane had no idea where to put his thoughts.

Even when he'd gone back into the gym to finish his lifting, he'd had a difficult time keeping his focus. He'd gone to his office to catch up on emails, but found himself staring at the same subject line for ten minutes.

Nothing had exorcised that woman from his mind and he had nobody to blame but himself.

He hadn't heard or seen Nora since she made her dramatic exit. Part of him wanted to applaud her for being so assertive, but the other part hated how she could stir so many sensations within him. In the years he'd known her, he'd only seen her professional and fun sides. She'd always had a smile on her face, always seemed so full of life and eager to shine her light onto others. She made an excellent employee, and their outside friendship had grown over the years.

Perhaps that's what had gutted him when he'd seen her so upset at the office after losing her dog. Her actions that night had been so out of character and had caught him off guard. He'd let that pent-up passion and years of desire override his common sense. Now Nora and their child were stuck with a man who could offer nothing but a financial commitment.

Zane made his way to the second floor and eyed her door at the end of the hall. Was she in there working? Fuming? Plotting new ways to drive him out of his mind with those sexy curves?

He ran a hand over the back of his neck in a vain attempt to release some tension. He'd have to get into the office to get any work done. Staying here all day would only drive him mad. He'd hang around each morning to make sure she was okay, but once she felt fine, he'd have to remove himself. The only way to get over this roller coaster of hormones would be to get back to the relationship they had before she ever walked into his office that night. The sooner they could regroup and shift their focus from attraction back to business and friendship, the better.

Nora's door opened and she stepped out as he still remained in the hall like some creeper. She jumped when her eyes met his.

"I was just going to go grab something to eat," she told him, closing her door behind her. "I assume you don't care if I make myself at home in your kitchen."

Someone should, because he didn't know how to cook and if it weren't for his chef, who came in once a week, that room would never be used.

"Everything here is yours," he stated. "I don't want to make any of this uncomfortable for you."

She took a step, then another, toward him. Zane didn't move, didn't know what he should be bracing himself for here. Was she still upset over the kiss? Or was she still turned on? Because there was no way in hell she hadn't been affected.

"I didn't mean to snap at you earlier."

She reached out, placing her hand on his arm in a gesture she'd done countless times before, but her touch meant too much now. He wanted more...and that was impossible.

"We both got caught up in the moment again," she went on. "And then your dad called, which clearly didn't help your mood."

Maybe he shouldn't be angry that Barrett had called. The man had very likely thwarted another bad decision. He'd called to ask if Zane and Cruz would be open to a dinner at his house, but Barrett Westbrook asked for too much. After so many years of neglect and selfish actions by his father, Zane couldn't forgive and forget quite as easily as his brother.

"Do you want to talk about it?"

That hand on his arm coupled with her sincere question stirred something deep inside him. He wanted nothing to do with deeper emotions; they scared the hell out of him. Not something he'd ever admit, but he had to at least be honest with himself. He'd had to shut down that emotional tunnel from his head to his heart long ago. Nothing and no one could reopen that channel.

"No."

Nora flinched and dropped her hand. "Despite what's going on between us, we're still friends. At least, I hope we are."

Friends. Right. Only he never kissed his friends the way he kissed Nora, and he sure as hell never slept with his friends. Was there a label for that narrow swatch between friends and lovers? Because that's where they'd landed and he wasn't sure which way they would ultimately fall.

"No matter what we are, I won't talk about Barrett."

Her eyes searched his for a moment before she offered a curt nod and stepped back. That instant wall of division slid between them and he knew he'd hurt her feelings. Still, he couldn't go there. Opening up old wounds and pouring his heart out had never been his style, and attempting to let Nora into that part of his world would only pull them closer together…which would give her the wrong impression. He wasn't ready to share his life with anyone—he never would be. He didn't need someone to talk to when he bottled up memories he never wanted to face.

"Fair enough," she replied. "I'll be in the kitchen. Why don't you send me all the information on that wedding project and I'll make sure the photographer, dresses, and other variables are lined up. I'll even *consider* the modeling gig."

Straight back into work mode. He should love that she went there, but instead, he had an uneasy feeling in the pit in his stomach.

Zane started to reach for her. "Nora—"

She turned to head toward the steps. "Email me."

Frozen in place, Zane watched until she descended the steps and was out of his line of sight. He'd wanted to get back to business between them, right? Isn't that what she'd focused on? What the hell did he have to be angry about when she'd merely done what he'd told her to do?

Zane had never had more conflicted feelings in his entire life. He'd always known what he wanted and had a clear path on how to achieve his goals. But now, with Nora expecting his child and living under the same roof, all he could think about was having her in his bed.

Five

Nora had to admit, working on the heated patio in her house slippers did have some perks. She had dressed for the office from the waist up, with her favorite scoop-neck green sweater and gold hoops. Thankfully, she'd only felt a little nauseous today, so she'd put on makeup, including a bold pink lip. After getting a tall glass of water, she brought her laptop out to the covered patio, where she could overlook the large in-ground pool, which was surrounded by lush plants. Spring would be here soon, but she figured Zane had his pool heated. The attached circular hot tub seemed rather inviting, but she'd read somewhere that hot tubs weren't good for pregnant women. She'd stick with her bubble bath, and besides, this wasn't her house. She couldn't just cozy up anywhere, despite Zane telling her everything was at her disposal.

She had managed to dodge him since last night, when he'd been so damn passive-aggressive. He either wanted her or he didn't. Apparently, he'd waged a war within his own mind, but his mixed signals were driving her crazy.

Keeping her distance would be her best bet. Each time she got near him, her heart kicked up and all she could do was let those memories roll through her mind. That night at the office had been one of the most memorable of her entire life. She couldn't help but want more—any woman would want another chance with the best lover she'd ever had.

The pregnancy complicated things. Living in his house complicated things. Keeping this life-changing secret from Cruz more than complicated things.

Too many variables went into play and her hormones weren't on the list of priorities right now.

Nora scrolled through her email until she found the one from Zane regarding the wedding idea. This could be a wonderful project for them, but she still had no idea why on earth Cruz thought she should be the model. That just didn't make sense. They had far too many other prospects in their queue or even in-house models who would fit this lineup beautifully.

As she read through Cruz's idea, she started making notes of her own. The grounds here at Zane's mountain home would be perfect. Something on the hill with a sunset in the distance would be absolutely breathtaking. He had horses dotting the horizon, various barns around the grounds, and beautiful fields that all looked like something from a movie set. The more notes she took, the more she envisioned herself in the role of model.

She'd hold out the full white skirt of the wedding gown. Her sheer veil would blow in the wind as she clutched a delicate bouquet and stared off into the distance. Her groom would step into the next frame and reach for her hand. Then Zane would—

No. Not Zane. He wasn't the groom of this faux wedding or any other type of wedding where she was concerned. They would have to find someone else for this spread. Her mind wasn't in the right place and she didn't want to have to play a pretend bride. It would hit too close to home that she might never be a bride—specifically not Zane's.

But she wouldn't go down that rabbit hole. Not now—there was too much work to do. Nora fired off several emails to get their art department involved. There were many layers to doing a photo shoot and they were already behind if the guys wanted to crank this out within the next few months. But her job had never been to question their decisions. The tasks they handed her weren't impossible, though some felt like it at times. Once, they'd needed a parachute image and she'd had to find a brave photographer willing to jump out of the plane as well. Nora hated heights, so just the thought of trying to get the perfect shot at the perfect angle thousands of feet in the air had made her knees weak.

After all the emails were sent and deadlines explained, Nora glanced at the clock and figured she had a few minutes before she had to hop on a call. That would give her enough time for a bathroom break and to grab some fruit. Zane had left for the office earlier, so she didn't have to worry about tiptoeing around him.

Just as she started to get up, her cell chimed. She glanced at the screen and contemplated ignoring the message. But she still had a job to do and she had to keep thinking of Zane as her boss and friend because, at the end of the day, he still held those titles.

She swiped the screen to read the message.

I've arranged a doctor to come to the house this afternoon for a checkup. Better to keep this under wraps for now.

She read the message again and the fury within her bubbled to the surface. Who the hell did he think he was just arranging for someone to come here? She had her own doctor and would make her own appointments. And even though they weren't telling people yet, his text sounded like they had some dirty little secret. Nora might not have been ready for a baby, but she wasn't ashamed. Scared, but not ashamed.

Firing back a quick reply, she wanted Zane to understand he wasn't in charge of her life and wouldn't be calling all the shots.

I have an appointment already with my own doctor and I won't be here this afternoon.

If she didn't take a stand now, Zane would try to run her life like his business and make no apologies.

Nora glanced at the time and didn't have much left before her online meeting started, so she'd just have to hope they didn't run too long. She actually had no plans this afternoon, but she would make herself scarce since she told Zane she wasn't available.

Maybe a pedicure or facial would do her good. Some self-care would surely perk her up and give her that boost she needed. She'd been so tired lately between the work and the pregnancy.

Nora sent a quick text to her favorite day spa and set her phone aside as she joined the meeting on her laptop. From the corner of her eye, her cell screen lit up and a quick glance showed Zane's name again. He could just wait. His message wouldn't be about work and she still had a job to do. A job he'd hired her for.

But when he came home this evening, they would certainly have a long talk and lay down some ground rules.

* * *

Zane had never missed more work than he had over these past few days. Skipping a couple of days to get Nora settled in, going in late to make sure she didn't need anything, and now leaving early because she'd ghosted his texts. He refused to allow anyone to simply ignore him, especially the mother of his child. He didn't know where this sudden burst of defiance came from, but he had every intention of getting her attention and laying out rules. That was something they both needed and he knew she wanted some rules set in place as well.

The more he thought about her not replying to his messages, though, the more frustrated he became. She claimed she wouldn't be at the house, but he didn't know if she just told him that or if she actually had plans. He knew she'd been on the meeting because he'd gotten a rundown of those in attendance and their discussion, but that had ended hours ago.

Zane pulled into one of the bays of his five-car garage and killed the engine. Nora's car sat in the circular drive, so he knew she was inside. He attempted to gather his thoughts and not just burst inside with his anger blazing. That wouldn't help anything, but she had to know he had certain expectations.

The damn woman drove him out of his mind with want and need, and now the fact that she ignored him had put him a cranky mood. The only person to ever irritate the hell out of him had been his father and, on occasion, Cruz. But now he could throw Nora into the mix.

He didn't want to delve too far into the idea that those closest in his life were the ones who could affect him the most. He didn't want to have trigger points that were easily accessible. Damn it. He wanted control back over his life—was that too much to ask?

Zane attempted to calm himself as he made his way into the house. He had no clue what he wanted to say to Nora, but he had to make it clear that he wouldn't be pushed aside simply because she didn't want to address their situation. She was living here for a reason and that reason was so that he could help her.

The silence of the spacious first floor surrounded him. He'd always come home to emptiness, but this seemed like a different void. He wasn't alone, yet there was still nothing.

Zane headed toward the second floor, and the moment he hit the landing, the clicking of keys echoed from her open bedroom door. He never liked interrupting work, but these were unique circumstances.

He stepped into her doorway and a punch of lust hit him hard at the sight of her sitting on her bed with her legs crossed. She had the laptop propped in front of her on a pillow and that mass of strawberry blond hair piled on top of her head. The cute little glasses perched on the end of her nose gave off that whole naughty librarian image, and he knew just how naughty Nora could be.

Zane pulled in a deep breath, clenched his fists at his sides, and moved into the room as he tried to shift his thoughts from fantasy to reality. Nora's head jerked his way and she eased back from her computer.

"You're home early," she stated, removing her glasses. "At least, I've always known you to stay at the office until late in the evening."

He stopped at the edge of her bed and slid his hands into his pockets to keep from reaching out. The anger from earlier hadn't dissipated, but the way she looked up and met his gaze had him considering moving this conversation to a less intimate room.

"Problem?" she asked.

"Yes. You ignored my messages earlier."

She quirked a brow and closed her laptop before focusing on him again. She shifted her body, flinging her legs over the edge of the bed. He couldn't help but imagine those legs wrapped around him again as he pleasured her. Nora had so much passion inside her and he loved being the one to pull out all of those desires.

Instead of getting lost in those fantasies once again, Zane scooted back as she came to her feet.

"You aren't going to demand I see some doctor I've never met." She poked a fingertip into his chest. "I've made my own appointment and I'll be going to the office. Nobody but the doctor will know why

I'm there and nobody knows about us, so throwing your weight around is a really good way to get me out of here."

Zane gripped her finger, gently easing her hand aside, but keeping his hold on her. Those doe eyes flared as she tipped her head up to hold his gaze.

"I want to be part of every step of my child's life," he informed her. "That starts now. I can't exactly walk into a doctor's office in town with you, because then the secret would be out. I can't have anything getting back to Cruz before I can talk to him."

"All the more reason to tell him now," she insisted. "Let me talk to him. He can't stay mad at me."

Zane snorted. "You think I'm going to hide behind you? I'll take care of talking with Cruz on my own time."

She continued to stare back and the silence, coupled with tension, seemed to envelop them, drawing them even closer. Her hand felt so tiny, so delicate in his. And those eyes never wavered, as if she dared him to challenge her again.

Damn, she was something.

"You're making a mistake not telling him now."

Maybe so, but he still knew his brother better than anyone and he had to make the best decision for himself. There had to be something in this situation he could retain control over.

"Will we ever agree on anything?"

Her whispered question shifted his thoughts back to her...and to the hand he still held on to.

Unable to stop himself, he reached to cup the side of her face. She had the silkiest skin with pink undertones, making her blush easily.

"We've agreed on things before," he reminded her. "We're not always at odds."

She tipped her head toward his touch, and the moment her lids fluttered closed, Zane had the urge to close the gap and capture those full lips once again. Nothing about that was a good idea, but that didn't stop his persistent ache.

"Didn't we agree we wouldn't do this again?" she murmured, looking back up at him.

"I'm not doing anything," he countered.

"You can't touch me and expect nothing to happen between us." She covered his hand with her own. "We haven't worked out any details with the baby or work or even Cruz. Getting more entangled would only add to our problems."

"Or we might forget about our problems for a while."

Why was he saying this? He didn't have the time or the mental power to try to keep up with a fling. And who the hell jumped into a fling with a friend, employee, and mother of his child? This pull of attraction consumed him. Just when he thought he'd regained control, something as simple as the look in her eyes or the way she tipped her head or parted her lips pulled him back in.

"Is that what you want?" she asked. "To forget the outside world? Because we tried that once and here we are."

Yeah, he'd tried to console her and assist her in any way he knew how to get her to forget her problems and give her emotional support for losing her dog. Seeing her cry and knowing her heart had broken had ignited inside him something he'd thought he'd buried long ago. For the first time in longer than he could remember, he'd wanted to comfort someone and take their pain away. But that first touch had opened a door they'd both tumbled through.

The one and only time he'd entered into a one-night stand with an employee...

But were they limited to one night? Because this sure as hell felt like something more.

"You seemed angry when you came in," she added.

"I was. I am."

Her lips quirked. "You always get turned on when you're angry?"

He always got turned on near her, but he couldn't keep exposing his thoughts or vulnerabilities. The last thing either of them needed was more confusion regarding the many levels of this relationship.

"Don't ignore me again," he growled.

She let out a soft laugh and took her hand from his to rest flatly on his chest.

"Then don't try to order me around like your assistant. I have no plans to exclude you, but the initial appointment is blood work and basic questions about my health. I can handle that part on my own."

Zane gritted his teeth. He had no idea what took place at these appointments. All he knew was that at some point there would be those little black-and-white photos of his child and he didn't want to miss when that took place. He didn't want Nora to feel abandoned or have her feel like she'd end up a single parent. Maybe he pushed too hard, too fast, but he didn't know any other way.

"Bring your doctor here," he told her.

"You make that sound so simple," she laughed. "You think you can just make anything happen?"

"Money can."

That's why he'd worked so damn hard to get where he was today. He'd gone too long without any financial stability or any way of holding power and control. His father had robbed them all of that foundation. The moment Zane and Cruz had had the spark of an idea for their future and financial freedom, they'd run with it.

"If you want to stay here for appointments, fine," she conceded. "But the doctor will be mine. So feel free to try to make that happen."

Oh, he'd make it happen. One way or another. He'd have to call the office himself instead of having his assistant do it, because every step of this had to be hush-hush. He wished Cruz would get home so he could tell him, but on the flip side, Zane also dreaded that conversation.

"Consider it done," he told her.

With that issue resolved, Zane should leave her bedroom. But they stood so close, with her palm still flattened against his chest and his hand still on her face. He didn't want to step away, let alone leave.

He thought she'd move, but her dark eyes remained locked on to his. Nora had a simple innocence about her that he couldn't help but soften to. But beneath that girl-next-door exterior was a fiery, passionate, strong woman he couldn't get enough of. He had to, though. Not only were they trying to figure out this whole baby thing, they were lying to Cruz.

"Are you staying?" she asked.

"Trying to force myself to leave."

She pursed her lips as her gaze dropped to his mouth. "You should go."

"I should."

Zane slid his hand from her cheek to her neck, then feathered his fingertips down the V of her sweater. She shivered beneath his touch as her lids closed and she dropped her head back. Her fingers curled into his dress shirt and his entire body stirred to life.

"This is a mistake," he murmured, still gliding his

fingers along her creamy skin. "Why do you have to be the one I can't stay away from?"

Nora slid her other hand up around his neck as she met his stare and offered a wide smile. "You seem upset over the fact you want me."

"I am."

She quirked a brow. "Then leave."

If she thought he'd back down from a challenge, she didn't know him well at all.

Only, she did know him. For years, she'd been his brother's best friend, his friend, his *employee*. And one night had shifted her role from all of those things to that of his lover. He should walk away, but he knew he wasn't going anywhere.

Six

She'd been irritated just hours ago, but somehow Zane had managed to flip her switch from ticked off to turned on with a few words and a simple touch.

Wait, no. There had never been anything simple about Zane's touch. His stare, the tone of his voice, the way his broad shoulders filled out his designer suits…every single thing about the man sent tingles through her. So how was she supposed to ignore how she felt? Even if she'd stayed at her place, that wouldn't have diminished her want. She'd had an ache for Zane for years, and since the night in his office, her need had only grown to a level she hadn't thought possible.

"I have nothing to offer on an emotional level."

Zane's words penetrated her thoughts and pulled her back to the moment. She released his shirt and looped both arms around his neck. Nora stepped in closer, pleased when his eyes narrowed and his nostrils flared. That muscle in his jaw clenched.

"Do you practice brooding in the mirror?" she asked.

His hands flattened against her backside as he jerked her body flush with his. "I don't practice a damn thing. You drive me crazy."

"Wow, so many compliments."

Zane lifted her, giving her little choice but to pull her arms tighter around his neck. Now she glanced down and there was no mistaking that hunger in his eyes. She'd seen it that night, she'd seen it yesterday in his gym before they were interrupted. So what now?

"You're not going to stop again, are you?" she asked.

"Do you want me to stop?"

Nora closed her eyes and tried to think of what they should do versus what she actually wanted. Clearly, common sense didn't exist when Zane was near. They shouldn't sleep together again, but at this point, what did it matter? They both wanted each other; not having sex wouldn't change that fact.

In lieu of an answer, she gripped his face with both hands and covered his mouth. She'd waited too long since that last kiss and had a hell of a time concentrating on work today.

Finally, though. Finally, she didn't have to hold back. Didn't have to pretend that she didn't want him with a fierce desire unlike any other.

Zane squeezed her backside and turned to sit on the edge of her bed. Nora instantly straddled his lap just as her cell chimed from the nightstand.

"Ignore it," he demanded.

Oh, she had no intention of letting anything disrupt them again. Whoever tried calling her could wait.

Nora reached for the hem of her sweater, only to have Zane's hands cover hers.

"I'll do it."

His fingertips grazed her bare skin as he slid the material up her torso and over her head. He flung the top across the room without a care as his eyes traveled over her. She'd never been tiny and had feminine curves, but the way he looked at her made her feel like the sexiest woman in the world. Clearly, he liked what he saw.

He went to the snap of her jeans and once the denim parted, he laid a hand on her stomach. Just that move had her heart clenching. She didn't know how they would work as parents, but she couldn't worry about that right now…nor could she change the situation.

But she could feel and she could want and she could take.

Nora took hold of his wrist and urged his hand

farther down. She didn't want to think about anything else other than his touch and finding out if they
were just as perfect intimately as she remembered.

"Nora—"

She covered his mouth with hers as she eased up
onto her knees to allow him better access. Maybe she
was using him—maybe they could use each other.
They were in this uncharted territory together, and
for a few moments, they could cling together and
find the most basic manner of fulfillment.

Zane slipped one finger into her core and Nora
tore from the kiss as a groan escaped her. She clung
to his shoulders and tossed her head back, letting
Zane work her body.

With his free hand, he reached around and expertly unfastened her bra. She shifted until the garment fell to the floor spontaneously, and a second
later, his mouth covered her breast. Nora arched into
his touch, completely consumed by everything he
gave. Her body started climbing and she bit down on
her lower lip to keep from crying out. How could she
be so responsive so fast? He'd just started.

Which only proved how potent Zane was and how
her body responded so perfectly to his touch.

"Let go," he murmured against her skin. "I want
to watch."

That husky, sultry tone of his, coupled with all
the ways he'd brought her body to life, had Nora re-
leasing the cry of pleasure she'd been holding in.

She didn't want to hold back, not with Zane. Even though they'd only had that one night before now, they shared a connection that went beyond the pregnancy. Their friendship had forged their bond and his compassion had sent her heart flipping out of that friendship zone.

No. She couldn't allow her heart to flip again. She didn't have time for that, and he'd made it clear he wanted nothing to do with feelings.

Nora came undone, and all thoughts vanished as wave after wave consumed her. Zane's hands seemed to be all over her, and she met his gaze as he focused on her release. Beneath those heavy lids, he stared back with arousal, desire, and something else she couldn't quite put her finger on.

The moment her body calmed, Nora eased off his lap and came to her feet. She kept her eyes locked on to his as she finished undressing. In the rushed, frantic state in his office, she hadn't gotten to see him fully, and she wanted that chance now.

Zane stood and trailed a fingertip over the curve of her hip and to the dip in her waist. "You're so damn perfect."

Not really, but he made her feel that way and that's all that mattered. He made her feel on every single level imaginable, both physically and emotionally.

"I'm also the only one not wearing clothes," she countered with a smile.

He gripped her waist and spun her around, lifted

her, then set her on the bed. Damn, if his actions weren't sexy. This entire situation had complication written all over it, but she wanted to hold on to this playful, passionate side of Zane for as long as she could. In a different world, under much different circumstances, maybe they could have something more.

Her mind couldn't even wrap around that concept because a life with Zane would never happen. Even if she wanted a family and to build a fairy tale including a happily-ever-after, he had made his stance perfectly clear.

"Wherever your mind went, come back to me."

Again, Zane's words and command pulled her from her thoughts. She shouldn't get wrapped up in the what-if game. She should focus on the here and now...and the delicious man who had started stripping down to nothing but excellent muscle tone and bedroom eyes.

Whatever he'd paid for that home gym had been well worth the money. She tried to take every bit of him in at once as he kicked the last of his clothing aside. But then he was on her, pressing a hand on either side of her hips and leaving her little choice but to lean back onto her elbows and stare up at him.

"I should have had enough of you," he muttered as he covered her body with his. "But I can't get you out of my every thought. You've ruined me, Nora."

His guttural tone told her he wasn't too happy with how she'd slammed into his life, but, hey, he'd done the same to her. So here they were, trying to figure all of this out together—their feelings and the baby.

But she'd "ruined him." How should she take those words? Had she ruined him for other women or ruined his perfect bachelor lifestyle? What exactly did that bold statement mean?

"Stay with me," he demanded. "Get out of your head and stay right here with me."

Nora slid her hands up his taut arms and over his shoulders as she parted her legs. Zane's body settled perfectly between her bent knees and her arousal started building at the anticipation once again. She should have had enough of him, too, but clearly she needed more. The ache she had deep inside her couldn't be described, so she wouldn't even try.

Zane kept his eyes locked on to hers as he joined their bodies. That instant sensation of everything being absolutely right washed over her. In this exact moment, caught somewhere between a dream and reality, Nora found herself wishing for this to be her life.

The weight of Zane's body on her as he began to move sent a burst of desire through her. Nora slid her legs up around his waist and clenched his body closer to hers. He smoothed her hair away from her face as he continued to hold her gaze. With one hand, he reached back and lifted her leg even higher as he continued to move.

The man knew exactly what he was doing, because those tingling sensations shot all through her. She held on to his broad shoulders as she met his thrusts with her own. Zane braced himself with a hand right next to her head, then leaned down to capture her lips. He consumed her from every direction and she absolutely loved every delicious second.

She bowed against him, taking him even deeper. Zane let out a throaty groan as he rested his forehead against hers. His hips moved faster and the build continued to rise within her. Zane continued to graze his lips over hers, but then traveled down her chin, the column of her neck, and back to her breast again.

Nora cried out as the emotions became too much to hold inside. Zane muttered something she couldn't make out, but it didn't matter. The climax slammed into her and she couldn't hold back another second. Curling her fingertips into his shoulders, Nora held on and let the euphoric sensation consume her.

Zane continued to pump his hips, then he stilled as his entire body tensed and shuddered against hers. Nora forced herself to focus on him, to watch him come undone as she came down off her own high. The man was positively breathtaking, his muscles clenched and eyes shut as he arched and continued to hold on to her thigh.

Nora didn't know how she'd ended up in bed with him again, but she wasn't complaining. Things were already complicated, so another round wouldn't change things.

No, actually this changed everything, because now she realized just how much she wanted him. Maybe she shouldn't, but she was human, with feelings that seemed beyond her control lately. Obviously, Zane wanted her just as much, but he'd made his intentions clear.

She had to be careful or her heart would get broken. She couldn't get attached. She had to protect herself, to focus on her career and her baby…and not ruin her relationship with Cruz.

Another wave of guilt threatened her, but she pushed it aside. She was allowed to be happy, and an intimate relationship, however temporary, made her more than happy right now. Maybe by the time Cruz came back, she and Zane would have each other out of their systems. She doubted it, but maybe.

Zane's weight shifted off hers as he rolled to his back and eased her over to tuck into his side. The silence in the room threatened to steal the joy of the moment, but she couldn't—and wouldn't—feel ashamed for being an adult with basic needs and going after what she wanted.

"You should move your things to my room."

Nora cringed. Those were not at all the first words she thought he'd say. Actually, she never thought he'd say anything like that.

Nora sat up and stared down at him. "I moved into your house—I'm not living in your bedroom."

Zane shifted, his brows drawing closer together. "Why wouldn't you?"

She couldn't help the laugh that escaped. "Why *would* I? We're not in a relationship. Everything about us is a secret and I'm only here because my place is being renovated. We're not playing house, Zane."

His lips thinned and she really didn't want to have this conversation while naked. Nora slid off the bed and started gathering her clothes.

"If we're having sex, you might as well be in there," he added.

Nora clutched her sweater and whirled around. "You don't want commitment, yet you want me in your room like, what? Your wife?"

Zane sat up, and that passion that had been in his eyes moments ago had been replaced by anger. "I'll never marry, but that doesn't stop me from wanting you. We both just proved again how compatible we are."

"I won't stay in your room so I can just be easily accessible, Zane." This whole conversation irritated the hell out of her. "If you want me in your house, that's fine for now, but I'll stay right here in this room."

When he continued to stare at her, she gathered up the rest of her things and moved into her bathroom. She closed the door and flicked the lock into place. Did he seriously think that, because she had sex with him again, she would just jump at the opportunity he presented her? Like she'd be thankful he wanted more of her?

What a jerk. How could his words be so callous at times and so tempting at other times?

Nora finished getting dressed and decided to contact her contractor. Surely, there was a way to speed up those renovations. Like Zane said, money talked, and she needed to get back to her normal life before she found herself wrapped too tightly in this web of desire.

Seven

Screwing up things wasn't in him, but he'd done a hell of a job since discovering the pregnancy.

No, he'd started screwing up the moment he'd invited Nora into his office and thought he could console her without touching. Because that first touch led to an innocent kiss, which led to not-so-innocent stripping.

He knew better. He prided himself on making smart decisions and keeping a level head in all situations. He'd always said he would maintain control over his own life and not end up like Barrett. He'd never be a half-assed father and ignore his responsibilities or put his own selfish needs above the needs of others around him.

Which meant he had to concentrate here. He had to put Nora and their baby above all else, no matter how damn much he wanted her. Indulging in sex with her epitomized the selfish side of him, the gene Zane had inherited from Barrett that he tried so damn hard to correct.

Zane slammed a hand down onto the edge of the balcony. He'd tried to keep his distance from Nora, but at some point, they were going to have to talk. That's what he'd been trying to do earlier, but she'd turned something inside him. His entire world had been flipped since that one night. Before then, he'd done a good job of keeping his attraction under wraps. He'd dated, nothing serious, and ignored the details when she'd talk about her dates.

Had she been attracted to him before that night? She had to have been or she wouldn't have become such a willing participant.

Attraction was one thing, but anything more would cause even more problems. He'd meant it when he'd told her he had nothing else to offer but financial support...at least for her. He had no idea how the hell to be a father, but he had to at least try. He would never want to make a child feel lost or alone.

He didn't want Nora to feel that way, either. While he'd never planned to have a wife or children, he wouldn't abandon his duties or responsibilities. He just wished like hell he could do more, because she deserved that fairy-tale lifestyle. The vibrant light that had always shined from her had diminished since she'd moved here. She certainly had just as much fire and strength as ever, but he missed her smiles and laughter. Had he stolen those emotions from her?

No doubt, Cruz would pick up on that the moment he got back into town, which was why Zane needed to get to him first.

His cell vibrated in his pocket. Zane eased back from the rail and pulled out the phone, not really in the mood to talk to anybody, but being the CEO of a multibillion-dollar company didn't give him the luxury to ignore calls.

Nora's name popped up on the screen, and he didn't know whether to laugh or be irritated, considering she was across the hall.

He swiped the screen and answered. "Nora."

"I figured calling would be safer than coming to your room to discuss work," she told him.

Again, he didn't know whether to be amused or annoyed. She had a valid point, but on the other hand, he wouldn't mind her coming to his room. Though she'd made it perfectly clear that she had no intention of staying in his house, especially in his bed. He'd been a convenient moment for her, and something about that fact really pissed him off. He'd never wanted commitment before, still didn't, but he also didn't want to be so casual with the woman carrying his child.

"Are you listening?"

Nora's sharp tone pulled him from his wayward thoughts.

"I'm here, but we can meet in the hallway or even go to my office. There's no need to call."

"Oh, there's every need, and I'm already in my pajamas, so I'll stay in my room," she informed him.

What did she sleep in? Something slinky and sexy to hug those curves? Maybe she slept with nothing but the cool sheets gliding over her bare skin.

Zane's body stirred at the mental image and he forced himself to concentrate on her words. He was a professional, damn it. Nora wasn't the first woman he'd slept with, so why the hell couldn't he compartmentalize her? She belonged in the employee/friend box. But due to his lack of self-control and years of growing desire, she now had a new space to fill… mother of his child. Whether he liked it or not, they were bonded for life.

"And then the ostrich will be here for the photo session."

"What? Ostrich?"

Nora's low, throaty laugh spilled through the line. "I knew you weren't listening," she scolded. "There will be white ponies, but no ostriches, though that is a good idea."

There she went being extra again. He wouldn't put it past her to have some obscure bird on set.

"What's this shoot for again?"

"The wedding project you sent to me, remember?

I've got everything lined up and I just received confirmation about the photographer and the dress designers. Everything is set for this coming weekend."

Zane rubbed his forehead and turned toward the open doors leading into his bedroom. "And you're still modeling for this?"

Silence answered his question.

"Nora, that's what Cruz requested, and he's spot-on. You'd be perfect."

"I'm not a model—I'm in charge of social media."

"And you do a damn good job," he retorted. "For this particular project, you fit exactly the image we want."

"And what image is that?"

Did her tone drop? Did those words come through with a completely different vibe than the rest of the conversation?

The very idea that she lay in her bed talking to him about business made his attraction grow even stronger...as if he needed that to happen.

"The image we want is a striking woman," he told her, focusing on work as he was supposed to do. "A woman looking forward to her forever and the promise that brings. A woman who embodies power and beauty who is sexy at the same time."

"I don't think Cruz said I was sexy. He's like a brother."

"There's not a man with air in his lungs wouldn't think you were sexy, Nora."

"Zane."

He stared at his open bedroom door through the hallway to her closed door. He only had to take a few short steps and he could be in there. She wouldn't deny him, not when she had the same crushing need.

"I'm stating facts. You're the perfect woman for this project, Nora." He pulled in a deep breath and continued staring at her door, willing her to come out. "You can look at the images first. If you absolutely hate them, we won't use them."

Why had he said that? They didn't have the time to do another shoot, they were already down to the wire as it was. Cruz's idea was brilliant, but had he thought of this even a month ago, they all wouldn't be so crunched for time.

But Zane wanted Nora to be comfortable. More than that, he wanted her to see what everyone else saw…her unabashed beauty and sex appeal.

"Fine."

He blinked, glancing away from her door as her answer came through.

"I'll do it, but I get final say on the shots that will be used."

Zane couldn't help but smile. He would make damn sure she loved those photos so much that she'd have a difficult time choosing which ones she wanted to use.

"You'll be thanking us later," he promised.

"I doubt I'll be doing that, I—"

A loud crash echoed both through the phone and across the hall. Zane dropped his cell and darted to her room, heart pounding, as he threw open the door.

Nora sat on the floor with a broken teacup in pieces all around her. Her eyes met his as she placed a hand on her nightstand and started to rise.

"Sorry about that," she told him. "I owe you a cup."

"Don't move," he commanded. "You'll cut yourself."

Zane carefully stepped around the shards, though some still crunched beneath his shoe. He reached down and lifted her with one hand supporting her back and the other behind her knees.

"Did you get cut?" he asked, moving to the other side of the room to place her on the chaise near her own balcony doors.

"No, I'm just clumsy." She shoved a mass of strawberry blond curls away from her face and peered up. "I didn't mean to scare you. I'd just finished my tea and was trying to set it on the nightstand. Clearly, I missed."

Scare him? Try terrify. He didn't know if his heart rate would ever get back to normal.

He rubbed the back of his neck, attempting to get his breathing under control.

"Hey." Nora came to her feet and flattened a hand against his heart. "You're fine. I'm fine. The baby is fine. I just dropped a cup and tumbled off the bed trying to save it."

Her calming tone did wonders for his nerves and he had no idea how she could be so convincing. Zane stared into her wide eyes and a stirring sensation wound its way through his chest, way too damn close to his heart.

But then he noticed what she wore…or didn't.

A silky cami exposing a few inches of her abdomen and a pair of little matching shorts had his heart beating erratically for a whole other reason. He'd been across the hall wondering what she wore, and now that he knew, he almost wished he'd never seen her this way.

True, he'd seen her completely bare, and touched and tasted every inch of her, but having her before him in such a seductive, yet almost innocent, manner seemed so much more intimate than sex.

But his thoughts bounced between his attraction to Nora and the flashbacks to his childhood. Another woman, another time.

"You good now?" she asked, clearly oblivious to his thoughts.

No, he wasn't good. A ball of dread formed in the pit of his stomach. Now that he knew Nora was safe, the adrenaline rushed from his system. Zane closed his eyes and forced himself to take a deep breath, then another.

Damn it. Was he swaying?

"Sit down."

Nora tugged on his arm and he pulled his attention from the near panic attack to the chaise as she forced him down. Could this be any more humiliating? He'd stand up and clean the broken cup in just a minute, but he had to get his breathing and heart rate under control.

Of all the times to flash back to his childhood and have this crippling fear...

"Just breathe," she urged. "Slowly, because if you pass out, there's no way in hell I can lift you up."

Zane couldn't help but chuckle. "I'm not going to pass out."

"No, I imagine you're too stubborn for that."

Perhaps, but he'd already embarrassed himself by not being able to control his emotions or reactions over the past several minutes. Nora didn't need to see that the father of her child was actually vulnerable and had a legit fear of losing someone else in his life. This feeling of total helplessness had been the entire reason he'd banned any type of commitment in his life. His mother had passed, and his father had deserted them emotionally, which meant Cruz had been his only family for so long. Allowing anyone else in would only open up a gate he'd closed long ago.

"I'm fine." He blinked, focusing on her worried face. "Promise."

"Why don't you just stay there for a minute," she

suggested. "You're finally starting to get some color back to your face. Care to tell me why a broken cup got you so upset?"

Because he still had some pride, Zane stood and placed his hands on her shoulders. Her doe eyes met his as her lips parted in a swift inhale. No way in hell would he share the inner turmoil that had haunted him for years. That darkness inside him had no space here, or anywhere in his world, for that matter.

"I just worried you'd cut yourself," he explained. "That's all. I didn't mean to freak you out."

"I think I'm the one who freaked you out," she countered with a tip of her head. "And I've known you too long. You can't lie to me, but I'll respect your privacy. You should know that I'm a great listener— just ask Cruz."

He didn't want to ask his twin about Nora. For reasons he couldn't explain and didn't want to delve into, Zane wanted to keep his own connection with Nora. He wanted to have his own bond and moments that weren't shared with anyone else. Obviously, they were going to share a child, but he wanted something beyond that. Not a commitment, but moments and memories.

Damn it. Maybe her fall had gotten to his head. His thoughts were all over the place and confusing the hell out of him.

"I'll keep that in mind," he assured her.

When the silence settled into the room once again,

Zane realized he still held on to her shoulders. Letting go would be the smart move, and he'd always prided himself on being an intelligent man, but everything about her made him want to hold on.

"We need to get that mess cleaned up."

Her words penetrated the quiet and smacked him with a dose of reality. He couldn't just take her to bed anytime he wanted. That's not why she was here and Nora deserved to be treated better than some random romp.

"Stay here." He dropped his arms and stepped around her. "I'll get it. I still have shoes on."

He needed to concentrate on something other than all of that creamy, exposed skin and her silky pajama set. Why the hell had she packed that anyway? To drive him even more out of his mind?

Zane gathered up the large pieces and grabbed the broom from the utility closet on that floor. Once he was positive there was nothing left for her to cut herself on, he turned toward the chaise, where she sat perfectly posed with a wide grin spread across her face.

"What?"

"I've never seen you actually work."

Gripping the broom in one hand and the dustpan in the other, he held his arms out. "I work every single day, even on my birthday."

Nora tipped her head and snorted. "Not manual labor. I'm surprised you even knew where the broom was."

"I'm offended."

Nora laughed as she came to her feet. "I assume your cleaning lady has just kept you informed of where things are in this enormous place."

"I wouldn't call it enormous," he retorted. "But Charles, who is a man by the way, does communicate often with me. And, considering I built the house, I am fully aware of where things are located."

Nora shrugged and offered a slight nod, her hair falling around her shoulders. "Okay, then. My apologies. I just never expected someone like you to take on any type of domestic role."

Zane moved across the room, propped the broom against the wall and dropped the dustpan, before turning his attention back to Nora. She remained unfazed by the fact that she stood there wearing scraps of silk. Knowing her, she knew exactly what she was doing by making him suffer. His penance for persuading her to move in and trying to get her into his bed with absolutely no promise of commitment.

Yeah, he deserved to be punished for dragging her emotions all over the place. In his defense, though, his had spiraled out of control as well.

"I'm no stranger to hard work," he told her. "You know enough about my childhood and upbringing to know Cruz and I were on our own for a long time."

"You don't have to explain yourself," she told him. "I was teasing you."

Zane swallowed the lump of unwanted feelings.

He hadn't faced more of his internal thoughts than he had in these past few days. Nora pulled out so much from him he hadn't even realized he'd buried. Never before had he wanted to justify himself to anyone, let alone a woman.

"It's important you know what type of man I am, considering we're going to raise a child together."

Nora slid her hand along the side of his face. "I know the man you are, Zane. Maybe you're still trying to figure him out, but I know. I wouldn't have slept with you otherwise."

Her audacious statement sent a shock to his core.

"That night wasn't planned," he stated.

"Maybe not that particular night," she agreed, dropping her hand to his chest. "But the attraction had been there for years. At least on my side, so the moment was inevitable."

Oh, hell. Why did she have to go and say that? He'd never been one to back down from a challenge or risky situation, but having such an intimate talk with his brother's best friend put him in a position he'd never been in before. He'd always admired Nora for her bold stance and the fact that she spoke her mind.

Never once did he think she'd been battling an attraction to him. All these years, he'd thought the desire to be one-sided.

She dropped her hand and took a step back, slicing the moment with her actions.

"Which is why staying here is so difficult for me," she went on. "My need for you is stronger than ever, but I can't just act on that. I have to be responsible and think about Cruz, my career, and our baby. I can't be selfish."

Damn it. Hearing her be so logical made him feel like a complete jerk.

Zane took a step forward, but she held up a hand.

"Nothing else needs to be said. Good night."

He'd been dismissed. Nobody had ever dismissed him before, but Nora's unwavering stare and rapid pulse at the base of her throat were all indicators that her emotions were running just as high, if not higher, than his. He respected her…which was why he found himself leaving her room with more conflicting feelings and turmoil than ever before.

Eight

Nora kept dunking her tea bag in and out of the hot water, hoping to steep her drink a bit faster. She'd thought her nausea had ceased when she'd left for the office an hour ago, but the moment she passed by the break room and smelled someone's microwave breakfast, she nearly lost it right there in the hallway.

She'd made it to her office and closed the door, hoping to cut off that atrocious smell. Thankfully, she had a kitchenette in her corner space, so she could keep the rest of the world out until she regained her composure.

The aroma wafting up from the peppermint tea already had her nausea subsiding.

Her cell vibrated on her glass-top desk. She flashed

a glance at the screen and spotted Cruz's name. She certainly didn't feel up for conversation—work or personal—but she still had a job to do and a secret to keep. No matter how she might be feeling, she had to pretend like everything was perfectly normal.

Normal. She didn't even know what that word meant anymore and had lost touch with it somewhere between sleeping with her boss and moving in with him.

Her only defense was that she'd always wondered what being with Zane would be like and now that she knew, she didn't want to be without. None of that logic made sense, but her needs went beyond physical at this point. Zane did something to her, something that no man had ever done before. He gave her a confidence that she'd never known, which only made her crave him even more.

On a groan, she swiped her screen and propped the cell against her computer monitor.

"Was a video call necessary?" she asked, curling her hands around her mug.

"I haven't seen your face in over a month, so yes." Cruz adjusted his sunglasses and inched closer to the screen. "Are you sick? You look like hell."

"You have such a sweet way with words. It's a wonder you're still single."

Cruz laughed. "You know what I mean. Why are you at the office if you're sick? Go back home to bed."

"I can't stay in bed the entire pregnancy."

The second the words were out of her mouth, she cringed and set her mug back down. Nora closed her eyes and shook her head just as Cruz's jaw all but hit the floor.

"What did you just say?" he demanded.

Damn it. Between the heavy dose of sexual tension she'd been living with and the whirlwind of her emotions, she clearly wasn't thinking straight. She waved a hand, dismissing his question.

"Nothing," she stated. "Forget I said anything."

"Who is he?"

Her heart clenched. She couldn't get into this now via a video chat with Cruz thousands of miles away. Zane had been firm that he wanted to be the one to tell his brother and she wouldn't go against Zane's wishes. That level of respect had to go both ways.

"Let's not do this now," she suggested, forcing a smile. "We can talk plenty when you get home, but nobody knows and I'd like to keep it that way for now."

"Did you tell Zane?"

Considering he'd been there...

"He knows, but that's absolutely it. I mean, I couldn't just keep skipping the mornings at work without telling my boss why."

"Nora, he's more than your boss. He's your friend, too."

Her friend, her lover, her roommate.

"I can't believe he didn't say something to me," Cruz muttered. "Did you ask him not to tell?"

"He thought because you were busy working and this isn't an emergency, it could wait."

An overwhelming layer of shame lay like lead in the pit of her stomach. Never in her life had she lied to Cruz. Their friendship had a connection deeper than most siblings. She told him everything and the one time she actually needed to open up and seek advice, she had to keep her mouth shut.

"How are you feeling?" Cruz asked. "I'm a jerk for giving you hell earlier."

Nora shook her head. "You didn't know and I do look awful. I perk up around noon, so I've still got a while to go."

"Why aren't you working from home?" he asked.

Another lie. She didn't even live in her home right now because of the renovations and Zane's persuasion. She should've stood her ground and either stayed or rented a place for the duration of the construction.

"I've been coming in late." At least that part was truthful. "I actually just got here and made some tea to calm my stomach. So, what's up?"

Cruz laughed and shifted his sunglasses to rest on top of his head. He took a seat in what appeared to be a park or some type of outdoor area with a bench.

"I honestly don't even know now," he admitted. "You threw me a curve I wasn't expecting. I mean, a baby. This is… Damn it. You're going to be a great mother."

Tears pricked her eyes as that pit of dishonor grew.

How could she be good at something when everything was based on a lie?

"Why won't you tell me who the father is?" he asked. "Is he a jerk? Is that why?"

"No, no," she assured her friend. "He's a nice guy—it's just that, well...things are complicated."

And that was the calmest term she could use to describe this chaotic mess she'd gotten herself into. Her eyes darted to her desktop. The last time they'd been in an office alone together, they'd been tearing at each other's clothes. Granted Zane's office had been the scene of the most heated night of her life, but still. The mental image of that first time together continued to roll over and over in her mind, but now she had another fiery encounter to add in.

Zane had gone from a one-night stand to her lover. Even though she'd held him off, she wasn't naive. Staying in his home surrounded by all of that sexual tension, in addition to their forged bond, was a recipe for another night of tumbling into bed together.

"If you'd let me in on your secret, I could help."

The concern lacing Cruz's voice touched her heart. He couldn't help her at this point, and if he knew the truth, well, she really didn't know how he would react and that's what terrified her the most. Not only did she not want to ruin their friendship, but she didn't want to come between two brothers.

None of their lives would ever be the same.

"I don't want you to worry about me." She picked up her tea and took a sip, welcoming the peppermint warmth. "All you need to do is find the perfect woman for our fall project."

"I'm actually supposed to be meeting her in a few minutes. I'm early, so I thought I'd give you a call. I did actually have a question for you, but I'll never remember now."

Nora laughed and picked up her cell as she spun in her white leather chair to face the wall of windows behind her desk. A slight wave of dizziness swept over her and she closed her eyes for a moment. Spinning in the chair was another thing she should add to the "do not do while pregnant" list.

"Can your child call me Uncle Cruz?" he asked.

Nora focused on his grin and couldn't help but get a flash of the future with Cruz and Zane playing ball in the yard or teaching the child all about the world of business.

"Absolutely," she promised.

She only hoped Cruz would still want to be part of her life once he discovered the truth. She couldn't stand if she lost him, but she would understand. She'd deceived him, and now she continued to lie. Maybe those things were unforgivable.

Only time would tell.

"What the hell, man?"

Zane sighed as he continued to scroll through and sort his emails. His brother's irritated tone echoed through his cell's speaker.

"Problem?" Zane asked.

"Why didn't you tell me about Nora?"

His fingers stilled over the keys as he jerked his attention toward the phone lying next to the keyboard. What the hell had Cruz heard, and how? Zane sure as hell hadn't said a word. And there was no way anyone could have seen Nora at his house, because he lived on a mountain with a gate at the bottom. He'd demanded privacy when he'd built the place.

"What are you talking about?" Zane replied.

"The baby. She said she's not telling anyone, but it's me. How the hell could she not tell me? Is she feeling okay? She sounds tired."

Zane eased back in his chair and tried to unpack his brother's questions. Cruz's only focus was Nora, which meant he couldn't possibly know who the father was. A sliver of relief slid through him, followed quickly by a rush of shame. His brother only knew half of the truth and not the most important part.

He wouldn't get into this now. Zane still stood by his decision to wait until they could speak in person.

"She's fine," Zane assured him. "She's tired, but that's mostly in the morning. I promise I'm keeping an eye on her."

He'd kept more than his eyes on her, but again, now was not the time to bring it up. Clearly, Cruz wasn't aware of Nora's living situation, either. Still, he didn't want his brother to know anything. Zane had wanted to reveal the entire truth at once, to have time to explain and have a future plan in place. He never wanted his brother to think that he and Nora were sneaking behind his back, though that's exactly how this looked.

Zane pushed back from his desk and came to his feet. The nerves and guilt wouldn't allow him to remain still. He paced around his desk and rubbed the back of his neck.

"Do you know who the father is?"

Zane cringed, but before he could respond, his brother kept going.

"I asked, but she wouldn't tell me. He better not be some jerk who only slept with her because she was convenient."

As if his layer of guilt couldn't get any heavier. Zane was exactly what his brother had described.

"She said he wasn't a jerk, but if that's true, then there would be no reason for the secrecy."

Oh, there was every reason for the secrecy, but Cruz would have to wait. Zane needed to get out of this dangerous conversation before anything else slipped out.

"When will you be back?"

"Not sure," Cruz replied. "I'm supposed to meet with a potential model this morning, but she's late. I should probably cut my trip short. I hate not being there for Nora."

"No need to cut it short. She'll still be pregnant when you get here."

And Zane needed more time before he crushed his brother's heart and damaged their relationship. Damn it. Every bit of this situation fell on his shoulders. The lack of self-control, the need to keep her close physically, but at a distance emotionally and all the lies.

He was no better than his bastard of a father.

Commotion filtered through from the other end of the line. "I think my appointment is here," Cruz stated. "I'll call you later, but keep me posted on our girl and take care of her."

Our girl. That vice around his heart squeezed tighter and Zane didn't know if that was the guilt or the fact that Nora had slid into the role of his girl.

"Promise," Zane replied, but his brother had already disconnected the call.

Zane stood on the other side of his desk and stared at his cell, as if he could somehow see his brother and gauge his mood and actions. This entire ordeal had gotten so far out of control, Zane wasn't sure if he'd ever get the reins back. At this point, he was the last person with the power. Nora held way too damn much where his emotions and future were concerned. But it was Cruz who dominated the situation. Every aspect of Zane's relationship with his twin and his relationship with Nora hinged on Cruz's reaction to the complete truth.

How the hell did this pregnancy get out anyway? Why did she tell him when Zane specifically discussed keeping everything a secret until Cruz got home and Zane could speak to him privately?

Anger settled deep within him, yet another layer

of his lack of self-control lately. She'd purposely defied him, as if driving him out of his mind with want and need weren't enough.

Working seemed like a nonissue right now. When his entire personal life seemed to be going to hell, he should turn to work, but his mind wasn't on any projects or the next board meeting. All he could think of was talking to Nora and figuring out what the hell was going on. The last thing he needed was the rest of the office to know she was expecting his baby.

Zane ignored all the warning bells and red flags waving as he stormed from his office and headed across the hall.

Nine

"Care to tell me what the hell happened with Cruz?"

Nora glanced up from her computer and relaxed against her cushy chair, meeting the very dark eyes of Zane as he closed, and locked, her office door.

"Well, good morning to you, too. I'm feeling better—thanks for asking."

Zane approached her desk and flattened his palms on the glass. "Don't play games."

"I'm not playing anything."

She shoved her chair back and stood. She'd be damned if she'd let anyone tower over her while spewing anger, especially the father of her child.

"The pregnancy slipped out," she explained. "I

didn't mean to say a word, but I wasn't feeling well and he picked up on it. That's all he knows, though."

The muscle in Zane's jaw clenched, his gaze locked directly on to her.

"Believe it or not, Zane. I'm human and make mistakes." She circled her desk and waited until he turned to face her, then pointed a finger in his face. "So don't barge in here acting like some Neanderthal. I'm your employee, not your wife or even your girlfriend."

In a flash, Zane gripped her finger, causing her to stumble against his chest. Nora's breath caught in her throat, not from fear but from arousal. The intensity of his stare, combined with the hard plains of his body and his woodsy cologne, had Nora grappling with why she was angry in the first place.

"You're the mother of my child and living in my house," he countered. "You could be my lover if you'd only give in to what we both want and stop being so damn stubborn."

She jerked her hand away and took a step back. She needed to breathe, needed some space to gather her thoughts.

"You think I'm stubborn?" she retorted, crossing her arms over her chest.

Zane's eyes immediately went to the scoop of her blouse, and that invisible sizzle between them increased. He'd never looked at her like this before, and she would have noticed because she'd been staring at him plenty over the years.

"You're impossible," she went on. "Insist I move into your house, seduce me, then think I'll just hop into your bed but not get attached?"

"I'm not in here to talk about our sleeping arrangements," he fired back. "I'm here to make sure nothing else gets said until I can talk to Cruz. I don't want the office finding out our secret."

"Well, I did just send out a special company-wide newsletter."

Zane's eyes narrowed, his lips thinned.

"Don't make stupid comments if you don't want them thrown back at you," she told him.

He stared at her another long moment before propping his hands on his narrow hips and glancing around the office.

"I can't do this," he murmured, his focus still on the desk. "I can't keep living a lie to Cruz and trying to battle my desire to have you at every waking moment."

Nora remained still, afraid that if she moved, she'd reach for him and they'd end up clearing that glass top of her desk like they'd done with his.

She needed to hear him out, needed to know his thoughts. Above all, she needed to focus.

"You know I can't give you what you deserve, but damn it, that doesn't stop this ache I have for you."

Only his eyes lifted to her and the turmoil staring

back at her had her heart clenching. The internal war he waged with himself wasn't something she understood; he wouldn't allow that. But maybe she could help if she knew what he was dealing with.

"Why don't you let me decide what I deserve?" she suggested. "And tell me what has you so desperate to hold on to these fears you keep hidden? I know enough to understand that you and your father don't get along, and I know you lost your mother. Let me in, Zane. Let someone in to help you."

Whatever she'd seen in his eyes vanished in an instant, replaced by determination, as he stood straight up and squared his broad shoulders.

"I don't need help with my past," he growled. "I need to figure out my present and how to make all of this work."

"You mean me? Because you can't have things both ways." She took a step toward him and dropped her arms at her sides. "You can't want me physically and push me away emotionally. If I'm in, then I'm all in."

His lips twitched, his brows drew in just a smidge. She assumed he wanted certain things, but wouldn't go after them for fear of losing control. He would never admit the impact his mother's death and his father's abandonment had on his life. Cruz had hinted that Zane took those tragedies the hardest.

"If we're going to be a united front for our child, then we need to be in all aspects," she added.

His lips thinned. "I'm not looking for commitment."

"Commitment found you."

She wanted to be upset with him, but how could she be when he was clearly broken and didn't even realize it?

"And I'm not asking for a ring on my finger," she went on. "But when I sleep with someone, I'm usually in some type of relationship. I can't keep tumbling into bed with you, because having your child doesn't make us emotionally tied."

Zane stared another moment before nodding. "I understand, and I'm sorry I can't be more for you."

"No need to apologize for being who you are."

Looking for a lifelong commitment from Zane had never been her intention. She wouldn't even know how to work with such permanent feelings. She'd purposely dodged relationships for so long. The pain of losing someone so deeply rooted into your life could make a person hesitant.

But there was still something about Zane. Somehow he'd managed to push beyond her barrier and, while she was afraid, she also couldn't help but have a sliver of hope.

She wouldn't mind seeing where they could go with their commonalities and their sexual tension, but she didn't want to force him to be someone he wasn't and she didn't want him to be uncomfortable.

If he wanted to be with her, truly be with her, then he would have said something long ago. She didn't want a forced relationship—she deserved better. At the same time, she also felt that he deserved better than being trapped. Sex—no matter how amazing—would only take them so far.

Why couldn't Cruz be the father of her baby? That man actually wanted his own family, but he just hadn't found the right woman.

But Cruz had never captured her attention the way Zane had. Other than their physical characteristics, the brothers were nothing alike. Zane had closed himself off from life, afraid to feel anything on a personal level. Cruz, though—he lived his life freely, opening his heart to all experiences. When the right woman came into his life, he would love her with his whole heart.

"I know fatherhood isn't something you ever wanted, so I understand if you need to step back."

She didn't even know where that thought or those words came from. She wanted Zane to be a hands-on dad, but only if he wanted that, too. She wouldn't have her child feeling like an obligation or burden. She might not know a thing about parenting, but she did know about love because she had been so loved by her own parents. If they were alive today, they would no doubt dote all over their first grandchild.

"My child will never wonder if their father loves them or wants to be in their life." He took a step toward her until she could see the amber flecks in his dark eyes. "I'm not stepping back from our baby or from you. We just need to figure out what role I'll be playing in your life."

Yeah, that seemed to be their hang-up. Just five weeks ago, she'd been Cruz's bestie, Zane's friend, and loyal employee at *Opulence*. Now she couldn't even count all the titles she held, but she could add liar and deceiver, which were two she never wanted associated with her name.

"We just need to go back to being friends," she suggested. "We both want different things in life. No matter how strong our chemistry is, nothing will change our visions for the future. So if we focus on building a solid friendship, stronger than before, we can co-parent successfully."

She hoped.

He continued to stare, as if mulling over her suggestion. There really was no other option. They were at a standstill as far as what they each wanted and needed personally. She wanted to see where they could go together, but he didn't. Even before they'd shared that first night, she'd always wondered what a life with Zane would be like. The pregnancy just forced her to bring the topic out into the light.

She never wanted someone to be with her out of obligation. That arrangement would simply be humiliating.

Now that she knew exactly where he stood, she wouldn't beg or try to trick him into anything. Maybe

Zane wasn't the man for her, no matter how much she wanted him to be.

"You're fine with only being friends?" he asked with a quirk of one dark brow.

If he wanted her to plead, he'd be waiting awhile. No matter how much she wanted something, she would never set her pride aside and appear needy. Desperation was not a good look on anyone. But that moment had made her stronger, and she fully intended to carry that strength with her through this journey, no matter what may come.

"Perfectly fine." She smiled and smoothed a hand down her pencil dress. "Which reminds me, we have my doctor coming to the house tomorrow afternoon. Are you still good with two o'clock? There's going to be an ultrasound."

She couldn't wait. She just wanted to see her little baby and start collecting the pictures that would mean nothing to anyone else but her. Would they mean something to Zane, too?

"My assistant already cleared my schedule," he informed her.

"Great. Then if there's nothing else, I'm trying to pin down the location of our shots from the rooftop bar engagement. Our photographer has suddenly gone MIA."

"If you can't find a replacement, let me know. I can take care of it."

She circled her desk once again and settled back in

her seat. When she glanced across to Zane, he hadn't moved.

"Was there something else?"

He blinked and shook his head as if she'd just pulled him from a trance.

"I'll let you get back to work."

Only once he crossed her office, unlocked the door, and let himself out, did she finally let go of that breath she'd been holding. She'd wanted him to say they could try for a relationship; that had been the hopeful side of her. But the realistic side had known how he'd respond. Still, she truly did have feelings for him, and she had to admit that this level of hurt at his rejection did sting.

At the same time, she also had to come to terms with the fact that she had to put her baby's needs and stability above all else. The more she thought of her future as a mother, the more excited she became. Yes, this had to be the scariest path she'd ever been on, especially without her parents there to guide her, but there was no turning back, so she might as well embrace her new role.

Nora spun toward her computer and pulled up her emails. She still had a photographer to hunt down and other priorities to address for her job. Daydreaming and fantasizing about her boss and his mad bedroom skills didn't pay the bills.

And real life wouldn't always be this fantasy

world. She had a baby coming and a relationship mess to sort through. At some point, she and Zane would have to decide what exactly they were going to be to each other.

Ten

How did one woman make him feel all the things? Aroused, frustrated, foolish.

Zane was almost positive he'd covered the gamut of emotions in the past few days with dealing with Nora. And here he was, once again, at her bedroom door late at night because, clearly, masochism was a new personality trait of his.

He tapped on the door and stepped back with the box in his hand.

Foolish. All of this was absolutely foolish. He was like a child looking for approval.

Not too far from the truth.

The knob clicked a second before the door swung wide. Nora stood there wrapped in another silky number, a robe this time, in a shade of purple that did amazing things to her pale skin.

Her eyes darted to the box in his hand.

"Are we exchanging gifts already? We haven't even had our one-week anniversary yet."

Zane couldn't help the smile that spread across his face. That's the side of Nora he'd always known. The playful, joking, sometimes-snarky side. Was it any wonder she got along so great with his brother? They could have been siblings themselves.

"I hadn't planned on getting you a gift, but I know you need tea in the mornings and your cup broke, so…"

He handed over the box, really wishing he would have just left it at her door for her to find.

"That was your cup I broke." She laughed as she reached for the box. "I should be buying *you* one."

Zane shrugged. "I think you'll like this one better, and I wasn't keeping score."

Nora eyed him a moment before she took the box into her room and set it on her bed. He took a step forward to watch her reaction, but remained in the doorway. Any time he stepped into an enclosed space with her, intense moments ensued, and that's exactly what he needed to be dodging to save his sanity and try to respect her wishes to remain friends.

He leaned against the doorjamb as she lifted the white lid and gasped. Inwardly, he was relieved she appreciated the gesture, but outwardly, he remained calm. No need to show his nerves like some awkward teen with a crush.

Nora lifted the mug and held it up as she turned to face him. Her eyes filled and he couldn't keep his distance. He'd always known Nora to be fun, playful, strong. He hadn't seen her upset since she'd lost Clara, so the tears hit him in a way he hadn't expected.

"Don't cry." He crossed the room and stood next to the bed. "I thought you'd love it."

"Oh my word. I do love it." She glanced from the gift to him. "It's just, this is my first gift with anything that says *mom* on it."

He'd had no idea what to get her, but he'd skipped out of the office earlier and had driven two towns over to a store he'd heard his assistant, Will, mention having the best gift ideas. The boutique had certainly delivered, and thankfully, the clerk had taken pity on him when he claimed he was shopping for a friend and had no idea what to buy.

The white mug had a cursive font in dark blue that read, Best Mom Ever.

"You don't know that I'll be a good mom." She sniffed. "I could seriously suck at this."

A lone tear ran down her cheek and that vise around his heart clenched tighter than ever. Zane slid the pad of his thumb across her smooth skin, wiping away the moisture. He'd thought the mug was a little over-the-top, with a silly, generic saying, but the clerk assured him that any first-time expectant mother would love it. Apparently, she'd been right.

He'd been so damn nervous shopping; that wasn't his forte. But he couldn't exactly send his assistant, considering the circumstances.

"You'll be an amazing mother," he assured her. "The fact that you're concerned about it tells me so, but I've known you for years and worked with you enough to know that you tackle everything head-on. You go into everything with one goal, and that is to succeed. Motherhood will be no different."

"I hope so. I don't want to ruin my baby's life because I have no clue what I'm doing."

A feeling he completely understood.

"I got you a few different flavors of tea, also," he told her, gesturing toward the box on the bed. "I know you need the peppermint, but I also got a chamomile and lavender. If you don't like those, I can get different ones, or more. Just let me know what you want."

"I want you to relax." She offered a sweet smile as she held on to her mug. "I know this is all crazy and scary, but just try to take a breather."

Zane couldn't help but laugh. "Shouldn't I be telling you that?"

Nora shrugged and turned toward her gift. She laid the mug in the tissue paper packaging as she sifted through the sachets of tea.

"I imagine we'll bounce back and forth being each

other's support systems," she suggested. "Besides, it's likely more stressful now than ever because the news is still so fresh and Cruz doesn't know the full extent. Once everything is out in the open and we know where we're headed, I think we'll be fine. Not to mention, once I can get back into my house and we both have some normalcy, we can really work on a solid plan."

Getting Nora back into her house had been one of the goals, but he wasn't necessarily looking forward to not having her here. Which was absolutely ridiculous. He couldn't keep her in his home like some pet. She had a life before him and she'd have a life after, only, now, their lives would have to mesh in newer areas.

His ever-pressing attraction and gnawing ache for her would have to be stored in the back of his mind... just as in all the years before. He would have to pull up every ounce of self-control he possessed to keep her confined to the friend zone.

But where the hell would he put all those memories? Every touch, every sigh of pleasure or heavy-lidded gaze, every kiss? Where did he lock all of those away? Because now that he had experienced Nora on a deeper level than ever before, he'd have a hell of a time simply forgetting.

"Are you nervous or excited for the ultrasound tomorrow?"

Zane blinked and realized she'd turned her attention back to him.

"I don't do nervous."

Her lips twitched. "No, I imagine you don't, but even if you did, you'd never admit such a fault."

Hell no, he wouldn't. As if he'd ever tell anyone, let alone the only woman who'd ever captivated him and the mother of his child, that something scared him. He never wanted to be seen as weak or vulnerable, especially to Nora.

Which was why the fact that they succumbed to their attraction the other day still irked the hell out of him. He had to keep his resolve in place and his guard up to make sure that never happened again. Each encounter with Nora seemed to grow more and more intimate. They were well beyond sex and had entered into some territory he'd never been before. That foggy area screwed with his mind and made him question his wants and needs and all of the goals he'd ever set for himself. Suddenly, work wasn't the only thing he worried about, and that scared the hell out of him.

When she stifled a yawn with her hand over her mouth, Zane started for the door.

"I'll let you get back to bed." A bed he wouldn't be sharing ever again. He owed it to Nora—and his very sanity—not to. "I have an early-morning meeting, but I can call in from here if you need me."

Nora shook her head. "Go on in. I'll be just fine."

"You'd never admit if you weren't." He smiled as he tossed her words right back at her.

She slid her hands into her robe and tipped her head, all rolled into one adorable, sexy gesture.

"Never," she agreed. "I guess that's just another way we're so alike."

As if he needed another reason to see their commonalities.

Zane left the room, and closed the door behind him before he ignored her request to just remain friends.

Nora scrolled through images of the sample wedding dresses that she'd been sent and really couldn't focus. Her mind still remained on the sweetest gift Zane had delivered to her door last night. He'd seemed almost shy and unsure, which were not traits she ever attributed to him. She wasn't sure if he'd been cautious about gift giving or if the reality of the pregnancy had hit home.

Either way, he'd been pretty damn adorable. In the span of a few days, she'd seen Zane passionate, vulnerable, and reluctant. For years, she'd really only seen one side, the professional, serious Zane. She had to admit she found each part of him endearing and, well, normal. She'd always assumed he didn't want people to know he had human emotions, because he kept everything so close to his chest.

Nora focused once again on the screen in front of her and tried to envision herself in any of these dresses. To be honest, she'd always thought she'd be in love with the man of her dreams before she ever tried on a wedding dress. So trying to choose three for the bridal store to send over for the day of the shoot was proving to be difficult.

Finally, she selected three completely different gowns and hoped that something would be perfect for the shoot. She also hoped the bridal bouquets being sent would be large enough to hide her face if she held them just right. She still didn't understand why Cruz thought she'd be the best one for this project. She'd never modeled in her life, but she was a hell of a social media mogul. That's where her confidence lay.

Nora glanced at the time. She'd come into the office only one hour late today because, thankfully, her morning sickness hadn't been too terrible. But now she got to leave early for her ultrasound and she couldn't view it soon enough. She just wanted to see the image and hear that heartbeat. Some validation from her doctor that everything looked good would go a long way in easing her nerves.

She shut everything down and was just about to head out the door when her cell vibrated in her hand. She didn't recognize the number as she swiped her screen. Juggling her purse in one hand, she tapped the Speaker option.

"Hello, this is Nora."

"Miss Monroe, this is Sven from Boulevard Bouquet. I apologize for the short notice, but I wanted to call instead of email. I am embarrassed to say that the order of purple roses didn't come in for the photo shoot. We do have a lovely assortment of lavender dahlias and I could still make a dramatic arrangement, but I didn't know if your heart was set on roses."

Considering she wasn't the artistic coordinator on this shoot, Nora wasn't sure what to say, but she was the lead on the last-minute project, so she did have the power to make all decisions.

"Sven, I trust your judgment, as this is your area of expertise," she replied, shutting her office door and then locking it behind her. "How about this. You make up a purple arrangement and bring another one that is wildly vibrant and screams springtime. Sound good?"

"What colors?" he asked.

Nora waved at Cruz's assistant as she headed toward the elevator.

"Let your imagination run wild. The bigger and more extravagant, the better."

Sven gasped. "Oh, this never happens. I promise I will not let you down."

"I have faith in you. Can't wait to see these bouquets."

She disconnected the call and sagged against the wall of the elevator as it descended. Considering she chose three dresses with different features, it was only logical she had a variety with her bouquets as well.

She had no idea how this shoot would turn out, but if Cruz and Zane hated the images, that would be on them. This whole ordeal was their idea. Well, Cruz's idea, but Zane had jumped right on board. They were out of their minds thinking she could be a model. And why choose her? She didn't want to catapult to stardom. Give this opportunity to someone who actually wanted to be in front of the lens.

As the elevator doors opened, she headed for the main entrance and the sunshine. This would be a great day, and all she wanted to focus on now was her appointment and her baby. Worrying about a photo shoot days away would only steal the joy of this moment and she refused to allow anything to rob her of this milestone experience.

Eleven

Zane stared at the black-and-white monitor as he stood next to Nora. The doctor and nurse had set up a makeshift area in his den, and Nora lay on the sofa, her eyes also fixed on the screen.

The nurse maneuvered the wand around on Nora's bare belly and then stopped.

"There's your baby." She pointed to the screen, then tapped another button. "And here's the heart-beat."

The rapid thump-thump-thump seemed to echo through the room, as did Nora's swift inhale.

"Does everything look okay?" he asked, stepping in closer to the screen. "Can you tell the sex?"

"We can't determine the sex this early, but at the

next appointment we should be able to give you an idea of the gender if the baby is laying right and you want to know."

He glanced from the image to Nora. "Do we want to know?"

She laughed. "Apparently you do, so that's fine with me."

Seeing that wide smile on her face as she stared at their baby had a roll of emotions balling up inside him. Never in his life did he think he'd be in this position, let alone with Nora.

The wand moved around more and the nurse tapped more buttons as images started to print out. The doctor came over her shoulder and pointed, then murmured something.

"What is it?" Zane asked as panic gripped him. "Is something wrong?"

"Nothing at all." The doctor assured him with a smile. "There are just various angles I like to see and some I want to make sure get printed for you two to keep."

Relief spread through him as Nora reached up and took his hand.

"Stop worrying," she told him. "Everything is fine."

How could he not worry? For years, he'd kept his heart closed off and he was doing a hell of a job keeping himself guarded from Nora as well. But a baby? *His baby?* Only a coldhearted jerk could keep from opening up to a child.

The reality of the situation hadn't hit him until now and the support from Nora's touch eased some of his fears and soothed past wounds. How did she do that? She didn't even know the pain he held deep inside, yet she managed to reach in and comfort him in a way he didn't even know he needed.

All while carrying his child, maintaining her demanding career, and handling stress like a champ.

He was damn lucky this strong, amazing woman was the mother of his child. There was something about Nora that made him believe she could handle any situation and rise above to come out on top. She'd become invaluable in his life over the years and there wasn't a doubt in his mind that she would tackle parenting with as much grit and grace as she did everything else in her life.

Once they finished with the ultrasound, the nurse handed Zane a long strip of photographs, each one with a little peanut-shaped image in a sac. The doctor asked Nora questions and finished up the exam while Zane made the next appointment. After getting Nora's okay, he opted for having it at his home again, considering he wasn't sure who all would know at that point. Even if Cruz knew the truth, Zane still had a business and employees to consider. The CEO's private life didn't need to be fodder for the workplace gossip mill.

The doctor completed his exam and Nora adjusted her clothes. Zane went to the door and waited for them to gather their things. He didn't want to rush them out, but at the same time, he wanted that alone time with Nora. The moment they'd just experienced together had pushed them into another level of bonding that he hadn't expected. Each day that passed, he realized just how much closer they had become.

"I can show you out," he offered.

Once they were ready, he led them down the hall and to the front door. He held the photographs in his hand as he let them out and reset the security code. His cell vibrated in his pocket and he didn't even look as he pulled it out to answer.

His eyes were locked on the image of the life he and Nora had created and he wondered how the hell he'd be the man this child needed. He had no choice and he damn well wouldn't be the father his had been. Zane had every intention of stepping up, even if that meant sacrificing portions of his own life.

"Hello."

"I hope this isn't a bad time."

A call from Barrett never came at the right time, in Zane's opinion, and today of all days. The timing couldn't be worse.

"I'll only be a minute," Barrett promised.

"Fine."

Zane remained in the foyer, still going over each picture of his baby.

"When Cruz gets back into town, I'd like to have you both over. And before you say no, I'm only asking for a few minutes of your time. I know you want nothing to do with me and I know I don't deserve your respect, but I'm only asking for time."

Zane opened his mouth to deny the request, just like always, but he stared at those pictures of his child and something stirred deep inside. He hadn't even met his baby yet, but he couldn't imagine never seeing them or hardly speaking to them. He wanted a solid relationship with his child and wouldn't let anything get in the way.

Granted, he wouldn't drink, himself, and gamble away his entire life. There might be a vast difference between him and his father, but there was also a very fine line.

"I might be able to make it," Zane conceded. "Just text me the information."

Silence greeted him on the other end, and Zane glanced at the screen to make sure he hadn't accidentally disconnected the call.

"Thank you, son."

Barrett's voice cracked on that last word and a punch of guilt hit Zane hard. Other than at his mother's funeral, he'd never seen his father cry or get emotional. The fact that Zane said he might be available was clearly something Barrett hadn't been expecting.

"I need to go," Zane said, then tapped to end the call before sliding the cell back in his pocket.

Damn it. He didn't want to stir up that old emotional baggage, but at the same time, he wasn't the man he'd been just a week ago.

"Everything okay?"

He turned to see Nora in the hallway just outside the den. Leaning against the wall, she had her arms crossed.

"Was that your dad?"

"Barrett," he corrected. "And yes."

"I didn't mean to listen, but I didn't want to interrupt."

Zane sighed and started toward her. He extended the photographs for her to take.

"I don't really know what to do with these or if you want to divide them or make a baby book," he started. "I'm new at this."

She took the images, but never looked away from him.

"Want to talk about the phone call?" she asked, easing off the wall.

"No."

"Are you ever going to open up about your father to me?"

"We've been over this."

She nodded in agreement. "We have, but you can't keep things locked inside."

Zane raked a hand over the back of his neck. He didn't want to have this conversation again and he didn't need to face his past, especially in front of Nora.

"I met your dad once," she went on. "Cruz and I actually went to dinner with him about a year ago."

Zane jerked. He'd had no idea.

"Cruz never mentioned it," he murmured.

"Probably because he's trying to mend the relationship and he didn't think you'd approve."

Zane knew Cruz wanted to try to reclaim some relationship with Barrett, but he hadn't heard about the dinner with Nora. He didn't want his brother to feel like he had to keep secrets.

Damn it. Zane had absolutely no room to complain or question his twin's actions. Having dinner with their father was nothing in comparison to the lie Zane had been holding on to.

"I never knew Barrett before, but he was well-dressed and charming."

Nora's words cut through his thoughts and Zane studied her. She stared at him, almost as if contemplating his reaction or trying to read his thoughts.

"I lived with the man for sixteen years and you saw him for a few hours. I'm sure he was charming for that amount of time."

Nora blinked and took a step back. "You're right. I couldn't possibly form my own opinion, and it would be wrong in comparison to yours."

She stepped around him and started for the stairs. Zane turned to follow her, but she reached the bottom step and rested her hand on the banister.

"Listen. You are going to drive everyone out of your life with the way you are hell-bent on keeping yourself guarded."

Her eyes bored into his and Zane stilled, unable to look away from that fire.

"You want to keep me at arm's length as well, even though I'm having your baby and I know damn well you want more," she continued. "You better figure out what you want out of life. You can either live it angry or you can *live*. Nobody else can make that decision."

She headed up the stairs, and seconds later, the door to her room slammed. Zane stood in the foyer for about a half second before he followed.

She'd had her dramatic exit, but he was about to make an even more dramatic entrance.

Maybe she'd been too hard on him. After all, she'd had a good childhood and didn't really know what he was going through.

And maybe that's what irked her the most. He had a father here and chose to hold a grudge instead of offering him a second chance.

Her door burst open and Nora whirled around. "Wh—"

Zane gripped her face and crushed his lips to hers before she could even finish her word. Nora held on to his shoulders and opened, welcoming the passion that she'd been desperately aching for. She didn't want to wait for him to make another move—he'd made the most important one by coming in here and kissing her.

Nora started with the buttons on his shirt but grew frustrated and just gave them a hard yank.

"Whoa, whoa." He stepped back and laughed. "I don't think that's how it works, though your attempt was pretty damn hot."

Nora reached for him again. "I want you out of this shirt. You've been driving me crazy."

Without unbuttoning the rest, Zane reached behind his neck and gathered the material before pulling it up and over his head. He flung the unwanted garment to the side and reached down to lift her up.

Nora let out a squeal as he cradled her against his chest and started toward her door.

"Where are we going?"

"My bed. I've wanted you there for years."

Years? *Years?*

And he was just telling her this now?

"Zane—"

"Not a word," he commanded. "We're not talking about it."

That seemed to be the theme with him lately, but now was not the time to get into a heavy discussion or another argument. She wanted him physically— the rest could be sorted out later...much later. Because her very real feelings had crossed over from superficial to something much deeper.

And that scared the hell out of her.

Zane crossed the wide hallway and stepped into his bedroom, then kicked his door shut behind him.

He laid her on the made-up bed and took a step back as he finished undressing. Nora couldn't help but stare at his magnificent form. She'd seen it all before, but she truly didn't think she'd ever tire of such a gorgeous sight.

"I love how you stare at me."

When he stood before her completely bare, Nora offered a smile as she sat up and pulled her thin sweater over her head.

"And I love when you're naked," she admitted.

Zane reached for the waist of her pencil skirt and then started easing it over her hips as she shifted back and forth to help. He'd expertly tugged her panties with the skirt and tossed both pieces over his shoulder. Nora reached for the clasp of her bra between her breasts and rid herself of the final article of clothing.

"I'm positive I love you naked more," he growled, pressing his hands on either side of her hips. "I could look at you all day, right here, in my bed."

Feeling saucy from his heavy-lidded gaze and obvious arousal, Nora tipped her head. "And how does reality live up to the fantasy?" she asked.

In one swift move, Zane gripped her around the waist and maneuvered himself to lie on the bed with her straddling his lap. He smiled up at her as he held her firmly in place with those strong hands on her hips.

"This is the view I would dream of," he told her.

"You right there above me, smiling, willing and ready."

Oh, his words sent another burst of need through her. To know that he'd lain right here and thought of her told her that she did have power over this entire situation—and it wasn't just the sex.

Nora flattened her palms on his chest and leaned forward. Her hair curtained his face as she found herself enthralled by that dark stare of his. He might keep his emotions close, but she was starting to read pieces of him. He wanted more with her—he just didn't want to want it.

And if he'd fantasized about her for years, that was more than desiring just a fling, whether he could admit such a thing or not. Maybe they could see where this would go beyond the intimacy and beyond sharing a child. But he would have to come to terms with his feelings and stop dodging everything that spooked him.

"You're frowning, and that sure as hell was not part of my fantasy."

Nora laughed as his words brought her back to the moment. "I'm not frowning," she argued. "I'm thinking."

"None of that here," he ordered.

Zane lifted her slightly, enough for her to hover just above him. A naughty grin spread across his face, which only added to her anticipation and arousal. She shifted enough to merge their bodies, and his groan of delight and clenched jaw were well worth her keeping her focus on him. He filled her so completely, so perfectly, in every single way, and if he'd only see just how good they were together, maybe this could be everything she'd ever dreamed of.

Zane's hands traveled over her hips and up to cover her breasts. He took her in each of his large hands and slowly massaged her flesh as he began to move beneath her. Now she couldn't help but close her eyes as she let the euphoric sensations take over.

"Keep looking at me."

That throaty demand had her snapping her attention back to Zane, who continued to stare up at her. This level of intimacy, achieved by moving with his body while keeping her eyes locked on his, was entirely new and utterly beautiful. What had started out as them ripping clothes off in what she thought would be a quick and dirty session suddenly turned into something meaningful and perhaps even more erotic.

"You're beautiful like this," he murmured, sliding one hand up into her hair to ease her down slightly. "I need more."

Yeah, so did she, but right now, they were talking about two vastly different things.

She knew what he needed, what he wanted. She claimed his mouth as she pumped her hips faster. Nora propped her hands on either side of his head for support as she covered him with her entire body.

Zane's hand tightened in her hair as his other one came to clutch her backside and urge her on.

Her body climbed, but she wasn't ready for this moment to end. She wanted to stay right there with him, for as long as he would allow. But she wouldn't beg. He had to come to that conclusion all on his own.

Her body continued climbing and there was nothing she could do to prevent the climax from slamming through her.

She sat back up and cried out as she pumped her hips even faster. Zane reached between their bodies, sliding his fingertip over her core, fully maximizing the burst of sensations spiraling through her.

"That's it," he crooned. "So beautiful."

The release seemed to last longer than usual, but when her body finally calmed, she still had a need for this man and his touch. She stared down at him and the hunger looking back at her gave her another rush of desire and energy.

"You're the one who's beautiful," she told him. "More than any fantasy I've ever had."

And that was the truth. Zane shattered all thoughts of any man that had ever rolled through her mind. He epitomized every single thing good she wanted in her life and in a partner.

She eased her body up slightly, then back down slowly, over and over, as she watched him fight against his own release. His hands fisted the bed covers as he strained against her. Then she couldn't stand it anymore, either. She moved faster now, taking his hands and placing them back on her breasts. She had to have more. Would she ever get enough?

He jerked and cried out as he continued to hold on to her. Another wave swept through Nora and she joined him in their release.

Silence filtered through the room as their bodies ceased trembling.

Nora eased down onto his body, but he shifted and tucked her against his side.

"Stay," he whispered. "We can figure everything out later. For now…just stay."

As if she wanted to be anywhere else.

Twelve

"I used to wonder if Barrett ever cared about us."

Zane hadn't meant to let that thought out, but there was something about the dark that made him feel safer. Like if he couldn't see the world around him, then nothing could harm him.

But even in the dark, he knew full well who lay at his side. She'd stayed. They'd taken full advantage of his open shower outside, off his balcony, which overlooked his property below. Living on a hill surrounded by a forest sure as hell had its perks.

Now they lay in a tangle of sheets and blankets, legs entwined, Nora resting on his arm as she drew a lazy pattern on his bare chest.

She said nothing, likely wanting him to continue

talking. He'd never shared his past with any woman before. Hell, he barely talked about things with Cruz. Zane would be perfectly fine if he never spoke of it again.

But Nora's frustrated words about the way he kept his guard up had hit him hard. He had to cope with everything from his past before he could confront his future. His unborn child deserved the best version of himself that he could give.

"When my mom died, I thought the three of us would be a strong, united unit," he went on. "But as the days went by, I quickly realized she was the bond that held us all together, and without her, we just crumbled."

Nora's hand stilled, and her soft breath washed over his skin as she let him get this out. He'd never had any intention of filling her in on those gaps she'd asked about. It wasn't that he didn't think she deserved to know, more that he didn't want to reopen a door he'd sealed shut so long ago.

"Barrett gave up on everything," Zane went on. "Himself first, but then Cruz and I fell in after that. He couldn't even take care of himself, let alone two kids. He gave up on the ranch and that ended up foreclosing. Gambling and alcohol became his life. Drowning out the hurt. At the time, I didn't understand why he didn't care, but as I got older, I realized he'd just checked out of life."

"You lost both parents."

Her words slid through the darkness and collided with his thoughts. He'd known that, but he'd never said the words aloud. How ironic that she'd zeroed in on that turning point in his life and summed it up in a few simple words.

"Cruz and I were scared," he went on. "We didn't know where we'd live or what would happen next. We ended up renting an apartment above a hardware store. The place had one bedroom that Dad gave to us because half the time, he passed out on the couch. We figured if we wanted anything, we'd have to work for it ourselves. We worked a few hours a week at the store below, but we did odd jobs around the neighborhood, too. Cutting grass, painting, anything that gave us money. We worked anytime we weren't in school. Our grades weren't great, because we didn't have the time to study."

Her hand still on his chest, Nora pushed up and stared down at him. The sliver of moonlight creeping through the balcony doors outlined her perfect silhouette.

"You survived."

Zane swallowed the instant lump of emotion that threatened to consume him. He had survived, but he didn't know what he would have done had Cruz not been there. They'd only had each other, and Zane had never kept anything from his twin, so his deception caused an inner friction Zane had never experienced before.

"That's why you both are so successful," she went on. "You know how to work hard to get what you want. You're not only surviving now, you're thriving."

"Maybe so, but there's always that worry in the back of my mind. One bad business decision or one wrong move could cost us everything."

"Are you worried about our affair and the effect it will have on the office?" she asked. "Because I can find another job."

Zane shot up in bed and covered her hand on his chest. "Like hell you will. You're our best employee and the only one who can handle all of our social media. Yes, I worry what this will look like, but you're not going anywhere. We'd be lost without you."

We. The Westbrook boys wouldn't be nearly as successful with *Opulence* if they didn't have Nora. But he didn't want her going anywhere for selfish reasons. Still, he couldn't admit he was the one who needed her. That would imply too much and confuse this entire situation…confuse him. Because once he said the words, he couldn't take them back. He had to be smart about this, tread carefully, so nobody got hurt.

The stirring of longing and desire he possessed now went beyond his physical needs, but to what end? Could he even trust what he felt, or were years of want and an unexpected pregnancy confusing him?

He'd purposely shut down so long ago, he didn't

even know if stronger, long-term emotions could rise to the surface.

"We'll figure this out," he assured her, squeezing her hand. "We don't have to do anything right now but rest."

When she didn't move, Zane wrapped an arm around her and eased her back down to his side. Having her here, in his bed, had been a fantasy; he hadn't been lying. But he'd never thought beyond that. Now he didn't know how to guard his heart and without breaking hers.

"I'm glad you told me," she whispered, snuggling deeper against him.

"Me, too."

Nora turned from side to side in the mirror and couldn't believe that the first time she'd ever put on a wedding dress, it was for a photo shoot. She had to admit that this dress made her feel gorgeous, just as every bride should. But she couldn't get caught up in the dreamlike state the dress evoked. There would be no groom waiting for her out in the gazebo by the pond. Only a photographer, the art director, and Zane.

Thankfully, Maddie the art director had helped her into the dress and touched up her hair after the stylist had left. Maddie seemed to be a Jill-of-all-trades, which was a good thing because she'd really need her help getting into that next dress.

Nora pulled in a deep breath and smoothed a hand down the empire waist of the gown. Her stomach still lay flat, and she honestly couldn't wait until she started to see that bump. She'd heard the little heartbeat, seen the life growing inside her, but she wanted to see that physical change. Oh, she might regret that later when she had to waddle or couldn't fit into her clothes, but right now, she wanted to feel that swell when she covered her belly with her hand.

Nora set aside baby thoughts for now and made her way through Zane's house to step out the back double doors leading to his expansive yard. She bypassed the pool and pool house, following the perfectly placed stone steps to get to the pond.

She clutched the lacy skirt and glanced up to see Zane only a few feet away. She stilled, her eyes locked with his. He wore his typical dark pants and dark shirt, unbuttoned at the top and rolled up on his forearms. But for half a second, she could pretend he waited for her, waited to start their life together and raise the family they'd created.

Zane's eyes traveled over her, and Nora dropped her skirt as she did a slow spin.

When she faced him once again, he'd taken another step closer. He looked nowhere else but at her, and her heart did a flip. Maybe, just maybe…

"Perfection. Absolute perfection."

The clap and declaration from the photographer broke the moment and her thoughts.

"Sven brought the flowers earlier, and I think the vibrant bouquet will be stunning with that lacy, vintage gown. The sun is at a perfect spot along the horizon to make those colors pop and you stand out like the vision you are."

Uneasy with this entire project and the way Zane continued to stare at her, Nora assumed that the quicker she got to the posing, the quicker she could be done. She wished Zane had come inside to see her, that maybe they could have shared a moment alone, but none of this was real and she couldn't let her mind get wrapped up in some playful scene.

Besides, she had to keep her head on straight and her thoughts clear, because this photographer was also trying to make a name for himself with *Opulence*. No need to bring him in on the company secret, not to mention that Maddie was a longtime employee. She would pick up on anything amiss between Zane and Nora before the photographer would.

"Where should I stand?" she asked, gathering her skirts once again.

"Let's get some by the pond first, and then I'll have you change and we'll do the gazebo."

The entire time she followed directions and moved her hands, her shoulders, tipped her head, all of it... Zane's eyes never wavered. With every ounce of her willpower, she concentrated on her poses and the excitement from the photographer and Maddie. They would converse, then change Nora's position again and take more shots. Nora smiled when asked, but when they requested a longing look, her gaze immediately went to Zane. She couldn't help herself. He was just…there.

"Yes, that's it," the photographer said, moving in closer. "Stunning."

"You're going to make a gorgeous bride one day, Nora," Maddie chimed in. "Isn't she, Mr. Westbrook?"

Zane said nothing, and for the first time since she'd met him, she had no idea what he could be thinking. She'd never seen that closed-off expression before, not even on Cruz.

"I think we should have some with her sitting and that lace around her," Maddie stated, breaking through Nora's thoughts.

Nora did as requested and forced herself to keep her focus off Zane. Clearly, something had upset him, but she didn't know what. She thought they'd turned a corner since he opened up to her a few nights ago in his bed. She'd fallen into that same bed every night since.

But maybe he wasn't on the same page as her and perhaps she was naive for thinking he could be.

After several more shots, Nora cheeks started quivering from smiling so much.

"I think you can change into the other dress now," the photographer announced. "I'll get everything set up in the gazebo."

Nora gathered the dress without glancing at Zane

or waiting for Maddie's approval. She headed for the house with her ball of emotions and wondered why Zane stuck around if he was just going to be in a surly mood, because that had to be what his silence meant. Wasn't it?

She'd tried to tell both guys this entire ordeal was a terrible idea, but neither would listen to her. She could only assume Zane was having those same doubts now and likely running numbers in his head of how they could scrap this shoot while re-creating the project and staying on track and on budget.

A sliver of her had really hoped he'd see her in a new light as she came out in a wedding gown, knowing she was pregnant with his child. How foolish to think any of this could build a solid future. All she could do now was get through this shoot and, tonight, sleep back in her own bed.

Thirteen

What in the hell had Cruz been thinking, demanding Nora be the star of this wedding shoot? And how ridiculous had it been for Zane to agree?

Zane excused himself from the photographer, who was busy looking through the shots he'd taken. He stepped aside and pulled his cell from his pocket. He had no notion of making a call or checking emails, though there was still plenty of work to be done today. Right now, though, he needed a distraction because he didn't want to talk to anyone or check out the fresh images on the camera screen.

He wanted to erase the image of Nora as a bride for so many reasons. The main ones being that he could never be her groom and he already hated the faceless bastard who would.

"Mr. Westbrook," the photographer called. "I'd like you to see these so I know if this is the angle you were thinking."

Considering that Zane stopped thinking the second she stepped out as a vision in white lace, he wasn't so sure he'd be of any help.

"You might want to ask Maddie when she comes back," Zane replied as he turned. "She's the art director on this project."

But the young man seemed too eager to show his work and Zane still had to be a professional.

The camera screen slid in front of his face, and Zane endured as the photographer scrolled through image after image. There was no way in hell Zane could choose a favorite, because she looked radiant in each and every one.

Like a dream.

She'd been his fantasy for so long. Even trying to keep everything about her superficial hadn't worked. Somehow Nora had penetrated that protective wall he'd built. She didn't use her words, though. Her actions had slowly embraced every need he'd ever had, and some he didn't even know of. The manner in which she cared for people astounded him. She loved with her whole heart.

Wait. Love? She didn't love him. Well, maybe as a friend, but nothing beyond that.

Their intimate relationship, the baby, and now this wedding project clearly had made his mind a jumbled mess.

"Sir, were you thinking something else? Because we can start from scratch."

Zane realized the photographer likely took his silence for disapproval. Far from it. He had no idea how the hell they'd ever choose what photos to use. Nora might think she belonged behind the scenes, but that woman embodied beauty and shouldn't be kept in the shadows.

A sliver of jealousy threatened to spiral through him at the thought of sharing her in any capacity... which was absolutely absurd. He had no claims on her. She was her own person and could do anything she wanted. Part of him just didn't want her to do anything without him.

"These are perfect."

He finally found the words to assure the young man his work wasn't the issue. No, the issue was Zane's own confused state.

"Here we are."

At Maddie's declaration, Zane turned to see his art director beaming as she carried the long train on Nora's second dress.

If he thought she'd been stunning before, that last dress was nothing compared to this one. The strapless top left her pale shoulders exposed and did amazing things to the swell of her breasts. While the top conformed to her body, the skirt fanned out all around her. He didn't know technical terms for what she wore, but the elegant shape combined with the fun, swirling pattern all over the gown had him wondering if she loved it as much as he did.

Who knew he'd fall in love with a wedding gown?

That better be all he fell in love with. Mentally, he couldn't even fathom opening his heart so wide and freely to another person. He had nothing to offer, not emotionally anyway.

"Isn't this gorgeous?" Maddie all but squealed. "The lavender flowers will be stunning with this, but I think we should also try that bright bouquet to really make this dress pop."

Nora's eyes met his, and everything else fell away. Maddie and the photographer moved toward the gazebo and were chattering away about lighting and angles, but he didn't care about any of that. He only saw Nora.

Slowly, Nora moved toward him and she seemed to almost glide over the cropped grass. She'd pulled her hair up for this one. Some random curls lay against the side of her neck, but kicked up when the breeze passed through.

"I never knew I'd like trying on wedding dresses so much," she admitted with a nervous laugh. "I mean, I've never had a reason to put one on before."

"I hate to tell you this."

Her eyes widened. "What is it?"

He took a step closer, using every ounce of will-power not to touch her as he leaned in to whisper, "You're the most beautiful model we've ever had."

When he eased back, her eyes were still wide and met his.

"Don't act surprised," he added. "You did look in the mirror, right?"

"I did, but I wouldn't go so far as to say 'the most beautiful.' I feel pretty, but—"

"Not pretty," he corrected. "Stunning, breathtaking, a damn masterpiece. Why have we never used you before?"

Nora blinked as if taken aback by his declaration. Maybe he'd been a little extra with his wording, but every bit of it was true, and she should start seeing herself like he did. The most perfect woman he'd ever encountered.

"You haven't used me, because I do my best work in my office," she replied. "And don't get any ideas. I'm no model, though I have enjoyed the day. But I'm not like the women who are vying for the attention of *Opulence*. I don't need a chance at a dream job. I already have one."

He wouldn't argue with her now, but this sure as hell wasn't the last time she'd be in front of the camera, and there was no doubt his brother would agree once he saw these shots.

"If you all are ready," Maddie called. "Oh, let me help you with that train."

"I've got it."

Zane hadn't meant to volunteer himself for the service, but the words slipped out and now he found himself stepping behind Nora and gathering up the yards of fabric.

"Damn, this is heavy. How did you walk in this?"

Nora laughed as she glanced over her shoulder. "I love it, so it didn't seem like work."

Zane stilled as her stare found his and something hit him hard in the chest. Too hard, leaving him too raw and vulnerable.

Love shouldn't be work. He didn't work at loving his brother, he just did.

But the way she continued to stare at him had him wondering if he'd been wrong. Did Nora have stronger feelings for him? Because that would make this entire complicated situation even more difficult to sort out.

"Let's start with the bright bouquet," the photographer announced, breaking the moment.

Nora blinked and turned away, leaving Zane with mounds of material and his thoughts. He didn't want to be in his own head right now, so he better focus on this shoot. Only, this shoot was the entire problem.

He never should have been here for it, but he'd had no idea the impact seeing her in a wedding gown would have on his mental state. It was a damn dress. Why did he have to get so worked up over it? It wasn't as if she was actually getting married.

But when she did…would he go? Would he honestly be able to see her walking down the aisle toward another man?

The next several shots would be taken inside the gazebo, and there wasn't a doubt in Zane's mind these were going to be absolutely as perfect as the last set. He'd just pulled out his phone to give Cruz an update when Maddie came up next to him.

"I know this wasn't planned and it's rather last-minute, but could we get you in some shots?"

Zane jerked his attention to his art director. "Are you out of your mind?"

She laughed and shook her head. "I figured you'd push back at that, but hear me out. You're wearing all black, and if we just get images of you from behind, I think it will really be something special. You look off toward the sunset and Nora can be at your side, your arms interlocked, while she faces the camera."

Never in his life did he think he'd play a faux groom to Nora's bride. Fate had to be mocking him at this point.

"You're the boss," she went on. "But you did hire me for my artistic vision, and that's what I'm seeing."

He stared at Maddie and she tipped her defiant chin. While he appreciated her drive and need for perfection, he wished he weren't on the receiving end of her idea.

"Come on." She patted his arm and gestured toward Nora. "Let's go."

"I didn't agree to this." Yet his feet were moving.

"You didn't say no," she countered. "I've worked with you guys long enough to know you'll do nearly anything for the perfect spread, and this is it."

As Maddie stopped the photographer and started explaining her plan, Zane stepped into the gazebo. He'd had this built more as a focal feature than to actually use. He never came this far out on the property, never had a reason to.

"What are you doing?" Nora whispered.

"Apparently, I'm the groom."

She stared for a second, her eyes wide, then she burst out laughing. "You're kidding, right?"

"Oh, I wish I was. I'm supposed to keep my back to the camera, though."

She licked her pink-painted lips and clutched the colorful bouquet in front of her. "Well, okay then. Whatever they want. But if you're not feeling this, I can feign a sickness."

"If I'm not feeling what?" he asked, stepping closer. "Like I want to pretend to marry you? Like I don't want to stand beside you? Like this isn't driving me crazy to see you looking this damn gorgeous, but knowing I can't touch you? Oh, I'm feeling everything, Nora."

Her perfectly shaped brows rose and she sucked in a breath. "Zane—"

"We're all set." The photographer stepped into the

gazebo and started motioning where Zane should stand. "And Nora, you next to him, but face me."

"Let's change the bouquet," Maddie added. "I think for this simple, romantic look, we need the lavender for a classy feel."

Nora's arm lined up with his and his entire body stirred. Her arm, for pity's sake. She'd been sleeping at his side for days now and they'd done a hell of a lot more than touch arms. But knowing they were out in the open trying to pretend like they were just friends or boss and employee put an entirely different spin on the situation.

Between the photographer and Maddie, multiple orders were given: tilt this way, shift that way, hold the flowers closer to your chin. Basically, Zane stood and stared as the sun crested the horizon in the distance.

"Put your head on his shoulder."

Maddie's direct command had Nora shifting once again. The innocent gesture hit him just as hard as an intimate touch. She trembled and he didn't know if that was from nerves or arousal. Either way, he was here for her.

Between their bodies, Zane slid his hand into hers and gave a gentle squeeze.

"Yes, that's it," Maddie declared. "Holding hands is sweet, endearing, and like a promise all rolled into one. I love it."

The flurry of snaps from the camera and Maddie talking about how these were the best photos yet drowned out any silence.

"I can't believe you didn't pay for that ostrich," he murmured.

Nora snickered. "I tried, but none could get here in time."

He had no doubt she would have truly begged and offered anything to get an ostrich on the set just to get a reaction out of him. But keeping this photo shoot so simple and elegant was exactly the tone Cruz had said he wanted, and Zane had to agree. Still, having Nora pose as the blushing bride made him recall just how gorgeous her glowing skin could be when completely bare.

"What are you wearing under that?" Zane whispered for only Nora to hear.

She laughed, which was the exact response he wanted her to have. He wanted her relaxed and to have fun with this. Even though the whole scenario right now was a bit much, he didn't want her to feel trapped or like their secret was something to be ashamed of. Not the baby, she'd never feel ashamed of their child, but their ongoing affair. Being so close and even touching had to be just as difficult for her as it was for him...maybe more so since she was the one who faced the camera.

"Birthday suit or something lacy?" he murmured.

When she didn't answer, he went another route. "Squeeze once for nothing and twice for lace."

Two squeezes, not that it mattered. Lace or no lace, he'd find her sexy and more than appealing. Would he ever tire of having Nora in his bed? In his life? She added so much to his world he hadn't even known was missing.

He had to be careful. He teetered on a line that he swore he'd never cross, and if he let himself get too vulnerable, she could destroy him. Oh, she wouldn't do so on purpose, and if he got hurt, that would be his own fault for allowing it to happen.

As the photo shoot wrapped up and the sun continued to sink lower, the photographer gathered his things and left. Maddie offered to stay and clean up the dresses and flowers.

"I'm good," Nora told her. "This wasn't difficult to get into. You've put in a great deal of time already. I'll make sure everything gets back to the bridal shop."

Zane approached Maddie. "I'll walk you to your car," he offered. "There are a few things I want to discuss about the project."

Considering he was their boss, he didn't want to seem eager to be in the house as Nora was changing. But he actually did have to discuss some things with Maddie. She didn't need to know that Nora wasn't leaving, that she was temporarily living here. They could keep up the illusion a bit longer, until…

Yeah. Until what? That was the part he still didn't have an answer for.

Fourteen

"This is the room I'd like to have the closet expanded in."

Nora gestured to one of the guest rooms closest to hers in her house. She'd called her contractor to meet to see the progress, get a timeline and have him work on the closet space in the baby's room—though she didn't tell him she was expecting. She wanted to do the designing herself, but she did need the closet much larger to work with her vision.

"Let's see what we have here."

While the contractor took measurements and muttered about a wall being removed, Nora checked her emails on her phone. She had to stay busy. Over the past three days since the photo shoot, she'd done more work than usual. That time with Zane had hit her hard. She'd gotten into her own head, her own fantasy, about how they would live happily-ever-after and raise their little family on his estate.

If she didn't get a grip on reality, she would end up completely shattered.

"It's doable."

Nora shifted her focus to the contractor. "Great. And how soon can I get back in? Realistically?"

He shrugged and slid his tape measure into his pocket. "I'd guess another ten days or so. We haven't run into any issues, but that can always change."

Of course, but ten days seemed like a lifetime and yet so close. She needed to get out of Zane's place. She'd gotten much too comfortable and didn't want to think of his things as her own. But at the same time, she hated to go. She'd never felt more alive, more cherished, than during her time with him.

Would he ever let her in? Truly into his world? He'd opened up about his father and that had been a huge step. She knew that had cost him a great deal of emotional stress, but she had to assume that if he hadn't wanted to tell her, he wouldn't have. They'd shared so much since she'd moved in with him that leaving would be difficult, but would he think so? Would he want her to stay?

"Is that timeline okay?" her contractor asked.

"Oh, yes." She blinked and offered him a smile,

realizing she'd gotten lost in her thoughts once again. "Ten days is perfect, and I appreciate you taking on this closet last-minute."

"Not a problem. Get me the paint sample and the lighting fixtures you want and I'll get the room all set for your guests."

Just one guest, and she doubted her baby would care about the paint or the light. Nora still couldn't wait to decorate in there. No matter the sex, she already had ideas for each.

She said goodbye and headed to her car. She had to get back to the office and look over the next set of video clips for their social media campaign launching next month. After that, she had to meet with her immediate team on a few other ideas she'd had for the spring season.

She truly loved her job, and she hoped nothing changed with her status once her truth was revealed to the world. She didn't want any employees thinking she slept with the boss for favors or perks. Thankfully, she'd been with the company for several years and she was always seen with Cruz, not Zane.

Plus, Zane had proclaimed that she was the best at her job and wasn't going anywhere. She hoped that would play out once Cruz discovered the truth. She didn't know if she'd feel freer once the secret was out or if she'd feel trapped in a relationship with her boss and friend who wanted nothing more...while she wanted absolutely everything.

* * *

Her day had lasted even longer than she'd intended. All Nora wanted to do was climb the steps, strip out of her clothes, and crawl into bed. She hadn't realized how exhausting it was to grow a human being, but she could have taken a nap at her desk earlier had she not been so swamped with work.

But at least she'd marked several things off her list, and now she had a ten-day timeline for her renovations. She would have to call to get her new furniture delivered, but first she'd wait to make sure her contractor finished on time.

Nora gripped her bag and her keys as she made her way up to the second story of Zane's house. His car had been in the garage, but she didn't see him downstairs and she hadn't heard anything. Considering that he was a workaholic, which came with the CEO territory, he was likely in his office. Maybe she'd grab a quick shower and change and read or something. She hadn't had a chance to read the book she'd brought, considering that she'd had her evenings occupied.

Not that she was complaining. These nights with Zane had been the best of her life and she wouldn't trade them for anything. Aside from the intimacy, she knew in her heart that something deeper had formed, but could she trust all the emotions swirling around within her?

When she reached the top of the landing, the sound

of water running echoed out into the hallway from the room she used to sleep in. Confused, she followed the sound, and as soon as she stepped into the bedroom, she spotted Zane in the adjoining bath, filling the garden tub with bubbles. Candles were lit, and a wineglass filled with juice sat on a tray next to the tub, along with her paperback book.

"Well, this is certainly a welcome sight." She dropped her keys in her bag as she stepped into the bathroom. "Are you taking a bubble bath now?"

"You are," he corrected, shutting off the water. "Perfect timing."

He crossed the spacious bathroom and took her bag as he dropped a kiss on the tip of her nose.

"Where's the real Zane?" she asked. "You've never kissed my nose or run a bubble bath before."

He laughed, returning to her. His hands moved over her skin as he started to undress her. Nora wasn't going to argue that she could do this herself, but she was intrigued as to what he had in mind. Suddenly, she didn't feel so tired anymore.

Strong hands lifted her shirt over her head, then he carefully folded it and placed it on the vanity. He found the zipper on the side of her pencil skirt and eased it down. As soon as she stepped out of it, he folded that piece with care as well and placed it with her top.

"First the tea set and now this?" she asked as he started to remove her bra and panties.

"You've been working so hard and I can tell you're tired."

Nora snorted. "Is that a kinder way of telling me I look haggard? It's because I haven't put on as much makeup lately."

He straightened and took her face between his hands. "You're gorgeous without painting your face. But I can tell you're tired, and I thought you might enjoy just relaxing a bit. I know you like to read or you wouldn't have brought those books. And you can't drink, but I read that orange juice was good for pregnant women."

He took her hand and led her to the tub, but lifted her before she could step in.

She nearly wept as the warm, iridescent bubbles surrounded her. She sank back against the cushy bath pillow and closed her eyes, welcoming the perfect ending to a long, hard day.

"Are you joining me?" she asked, throwing him a glance.

"This is for you," he told her as he took a seat on the stool next to the tub. He held up the book. "Is this one okay?"

"I just bought it, but I love that author."

He glanced at the cover, then read the back before shrugging. "Doesn't sound terrible. Let's get started."

He handed her the juice and then flipped open the cover.

"Wait." She gripped the stem of her glass. "You're reading to me?"

"If you'll relax and just be quiet, I will."

She wasn't sure if she was impressed or still confused, but she wasn't about to ask any more questions. Taking a sip of her juice, she settled back in as Zane's low tone started with chapter one. This was like an audio book mingled with foreplay and very likely shaping up to be the greatest night of her life. He'd put so much thought into her needs and she'd had no idea he'd been planning anything. Here she thought he'd been working in his office.

She'd been dodging him just a bit over these past couple of days, trying to gather her thoughts since the photo shoot. She wasn't sure what answer she was looking for, considering that she didn't fully know the question, but she hadn't come up with anything.

Did she tell Zane her feelings had gotten stronger? Did she lay it all on the line and let him make his own decisions?

Or should she just wait and hope he realized that this could be so much more than temporary? Once their secret came out and Cruz knew the full truth, would Zane feel free to reveal his feelings? He kept everything so close to his chest, but in her own heart, she knew he had to love her on some level. His actions proved that their relationship hinged on much more than friendship and sex. Yes, their baby would always bind them together, but there was more.

Zane paused his reading. "Do women actually look at the size of a man's shoulders?"

Nora shifted her attention back to Zane as she set

her juice on the edge of the tub. "Absolutely. And yours are magnificent, by the way."

Zane glanced at the cover again, then back to her. "Better than this guy?" he asked, tapping the image of the male cover model.

"No comparison."

A grin spread across his face. "Good to know."

"Now, keep reading. This is the best gift anyone has ever gotten me."

Zane jerked. "I didn't even buy anything, so I don't think this constitutes a gift."

Nora shifted so she could face him as she rested her arm along the side of the tub. "I don't need anyone to buy me things. I can buy whatever I want. It's the gestures from the heart that mean more than anything."

His brows drew in as he studied her. "You're not like other women I know."

"You're just now figuring that out? We've known each other a long time."

"Maybe so, but I've never spent this much time with you and gotten to know you on this level."

On this level. She wanted to ask what level he was referring to exactly, but she didn't want to ruin the moment with an uncomfortable, yet inevitable, conversation.

"Keep reading," she ordered, settling back against her pillow. "Or join me—the choice is yours."

She closed her eyes once again, waiting for him to decide. The silence in the room seemed to go on forever as she listened for movement or his voice. She wanted him in there with her; there was plenty of room. She wanted to show him just how much she appreciated this night and how he'd thought of everything to make her happy and comfortable.

A man wouldn't go through all of this just for sex. They were already doing that and it wasn't as if he had to beg.

Finally, he shifted. The book fell to the floor with a thunk and the rustling of clothing soon followed. Anticipation and arousal spiraled through her and she opened her eyes to see him stepping into the tub. He sank beneath the bubbles on the other end and extended his legs on either side of her.

Nora smiled and laid her arms along the edge. "I never took you for a bubble bath type of guy."

"I'm doing a great many things I never saw myself doing before you."

She had no doubt he'd done a mental transformation since that night in her office. Neither of them was the same person. They'd started growing together, but would that be enough for something more? She believed so, but Zane still remained so frustratingly cautious.

Maybe now was the time to reveal her feelings. How could Zane make his own conclusions if he didn't have an insight into her true heart? He'd opened himself up to her the other day—now it was her turn.

"I'm pretty sure I'm falling in love with you."

Okay, so she hadn't meant to just blurt that out there, but there wasn't really a great way to ease into that announcement.

And from the silence and Zane's unblinking stare, she had to assume those weren't words he wanted to hear.

"I'm not telling you that to scare you," she added. "I'm sure you'd rather I kept that bit of information to myself, but that wouldn't have been fair to either one of us."

Again, silence. Her heart beat so fast, and she realized she'd chosen the most exposed moment for this reveal. Aside from their obvious state of undress, she'd opened her heart wider than ever before and she knew his still had those cracks from where he'd let her in the other day.

Someone had to bring out the truth so they could move beyond this stalemate and stop dancing around the topic. Now she wished she would have waited until they were wearing clothes, but at least he couldn't just run away.

"I don't know what you want me to say here."

His murmured statement settled between them and she couldn't deny that a tiny piece of her broke. In that perfect dreamlike world, he would have returned the sentiment. But this was reality and she had to accept whatever response he gave. The respect had to go both directions, and she didn't want any man whose emotions she had to pull out.

"I don't want you to say anything if you don't mean

it," she informed him. "You need to know where I stand, that's all. I can't lie to you, especially with all we've shared. You deserve the truth."

He continued to stare another moment before easing forward and resting his hands on her raised knees.

"Nora, I can't offer you more."

Pain laced his voice and she knew this cost him. She knew he battled some internal war with himself and had to be torn, especially now that she'd dropped that bold statement.

"I haven't promised anything, for that reason." Those strong hands curled around her knees. "I never want to hurt you and this is exactly what I was afraid would happen."

"I'm not hurt," she countered with a smile. "Love doesn't hurt. I feel fine now that I've told you and now you are free to do what you want. If anything, I feel bad for you for not facing your own feelings, but I can't make that decision for you."

Zane's dark brows drew in. "You're confusing me. You don't want me to tell you I love you in return?"

She wanted nothing more, but she would never beg or force someone into feelings they weren't ready for. She knew what it meant to guard your heart; she'd been doing it for years.

"In a world where everything is perfect, that would happen, but we haven't exactly lived in a fairy tale, have we?" She laughed, but her lame joke didn't go too far, as he still looked just as perplexed. "I didn't mean to ruin this beautiful evening you created for me," she added. "I just couldn't keep that emotion locked away any longer."

He rubbed his hands down her legs and continued to hold her stare. She wanted to know what he was thinking, but his lack of emotions really told her all she needed to know. She just wished he wouldn't be so afraid to take a chance. He'd taken a huge risk years ago when he'd started a business, and each step that propelled him further into success had been risky. Why couldn't he grasp that this moment was no different? They deserved to try, not only for the baby, but also for themselves.

"You didn't ruin anything." He shifted to inch even closer. "The fact you feel that way and you're comfortable enough to let me in is…"

When he shook his head, Nora maneuvered herself onto his lap and wrapped her legs around his waist. She looped her arms around his neck and moved in close, needing him to look her in the eyes.

"Don't say anything else," she whispered. "Let's just enjoy our evening and our time alone."

He looked like he wanted to say something else, but she didn't want him trying to defend his reasoning or saying something only to make her happy. There was no room here for half-emotions or lies. They had enough of that already. All she could do from here on out was be true to herself and how she felt about Zane and their relationship. Everything else would be up to him.

"I don't want you upset," he murmured against her lips as he flattened his palms against her back.

Nora tipped her head up just slightly. "Do I look upset? The father of my child has spoiled me and will do anything to make me happy. Is that love? No, but not saying the words doesn't make you any less caring. We're good, Zane. Promise."

He slid his mouth across hers. Back and forth, enough to drive her completely mad with want.

"You're remarkable. If I could love anyone, Nora, I'd choose you."

A flutter of hope burst through her. She knew Zane teetered on the edge of falling, and all she had to do was make sure she was there to catch him.

Fifteen

Zane had just poured a cup of coffee when Nora padded into the kitchen. She'd piled her hair atop her head and belted her floral robe around her waist. They'd shared a bed last night, but he'd lain awake with her tucked right against his side.

How could he sleep after she'd dropped that proclamation? She loved him? That was never supposed to happen. The oddest thing? He truly believed she was happier after telling him even though he hadn't returned the words.

How did that even work? Love—if that's what she actually felt—had to be the weirdest, most confusing emotion. Why couldn't they just keep on the way they were going? Agreeing to raise their child with the same values, continuing their fling because they enjoyed each other's company, and working together as they had for years?

Was all of that too much to ask?

Now love had entered the mix, and on the coattails of that damn wedding shoot, no less.

The driveway alarm echoed through the house as Nora took a seat at the breakfast table. His stable hands were running a little late this morning, he realized as he glanced at the clock on the wall.

"Do you care to make me some tea?" Nora asked as she rested her head in her folded arms on the table.

Zane crossed the spacious room and slid his hand over her hair, wanting to console her as much as possible. He had no idea what she was dealing with, so all he could do was comfort her the best way he knew how.

"Why don't you go back up to bed?" he suggested.

"I'll be fine." Her words muffled as she remained huddled over the table. "I'm trying to get going earlier, so I thought I'd push myself more today since it's the weekend. Maybe by next week I'll be somewhat back to normal."

He pulled a mug from the cabinet and went to her box of teas on the counter.

"You don't have the flu or a cold. You have morning sickness. Is that something you can just push through?"

"I have no idea," she replied. "But I'm going to try."

He tore open the peppermint pouch and placed the

bag into the mug, then glanced back to Nora. She'd sat back up and her eyes were on him now.

"I met with my contractor," she told him. "I'm having him work in one of my guest rooms to get ready for a nursery. So he said the timeline might be just a bit longer. I should be out of here within a couple weeks, though."

He'd known she would leave; that had been the plan all along. But after all they'd shared and after her declaration last night, was that what she honestly wanted to do?

"I didn't think you were in a hurry to go," he replied, resting his hip against the counter.

Nora shrugged and crossed her arms over her chest as she shifted in her chair. She crossed her legs and faced him, and his eyes went to those adorable pink-polished toes. So dainty and so perfect. But she couldn't be perfect...not for him.

"I'm not in a hurry, but it would be nice to get back to my house and start settling into my new normal. We can't keep playing house forever."

Maybe not, but until they knew what they were doing, why couldn't she just stay? He wasn't quite ready to let her go. She'd opened up to him last night, so maybe he should do the same.

"I want you to stay."

Nora blinked up at him as the driveway alarm echoed through the house once again. Damn, he'd have to start cracking down on those employees who lived off-site. They were coming in much too late.

"Why?" she asked.

The kettle whistled, and he grabbed the mug and moved to the stove in the island. He had to be careful with his words, especially after last night. He didn't want to mislead her or give her false hope. He'd been very clear from the start what he could and would offer.

"There's no reason for you to go." He started, but stopped when she let out a snort.

"There's every reason," she corrected. "The fact that we want two very different lifestyles would be the main one. I'm not here just to keep your bed warm, Zane. As much as I love our time together, I deserve more and, frankly, so do you."

He poured the steaming water over the tea bag and then crossed the kitchen to where Nora sat. He placed the mug in front of her, but didn't take a seat. He didn't want to get too relaxed, and he needed to keep the upper hand here.

"I'm just saying that there's no rush for you to go," he went on. "You're clearly still not feeling well and—"

"I'm doing better each morning." She dipped her tea bag and stirred it around the water, all without meeting his gaze. "I'm not asking you, Zane. I'm telling you that I'll be leaving as soon as my house is done."

Now she offered him her unreadable expression and he merely stood above her, not sure what to say next. He didn't want to piss her off or hurt her feelings, and apparently, he was doing both.

"Nora—"

His back door flew open, jerking Zane's attention to the unexpected guest.

"Cruz."

Nora's word came out on a gasp as she came to her feet and clutched her robe.

His twin brother's eyes darted from Nora to Zane, taking in their obvious state of undress.

"What the hell?"

Nora started to take a step, but crumbled. Zane caught her just before she hit the floor.

"Don't move."

Nora blinked up at identical faces, but even in her current state, and with the wave of nausea, she could still tell the difference between these brothers.

"I'm fine," she assured them. "Just let me get back to my chair."

How embarrassing to be dizzy and move too fast only to fall into a heap.

"I've got you."

Zane lifted her into his arms and started toward the informal living area just off the kitchen.

"This is really silly," she argued in vain. "I can walk. I just moved too fast and got light-headed."

When Zane placed her on the sofa with her legs extended, Nora adjusted the throw pillow behind her and settled in. She really wanted to stand, but her head was still spinning at the fact that Cruz had arrived on scene, unannounced, and clearly confused. She needed to remain still, to get control of her breathing, and deal with everything head-on.

Their time to come clean with him had arrived and she hated that in a matter of moments, their entire relationship would change. As if the morning sickness hadn't made her ill enough, the idea of ruining years of friendships terrified her.

"Are you okay?" Cruz asked, coming to stand beside Zane.

Two sets of worried eyes still held her in place and Nora offered a smile as she nodded.

"I promise, I'm fine. But I would like my tea since my stomach is still a little queasy."

Zane was gone before she finished the sentence and Cruz took a seat on the table before her.

"You look pale," he told her, reaching for her hand. "What else do you need?"

"About two hours and I'm good to go." She laughed and squeezed his hand. "Stop looking at me like that. I'm not dying—I'm pregnant."

Zane stepped back in with her tea and set it on the table next to Cruz.

"Stay here," Zane told her. "I'm going to talk to Cruz in the other room."

Nora stared for a second before she laughed. "You're joking, right? You think I'm just going to sit here like an obedient dog? Nice try."

Cruz glanced up to his brother. "You both can tell me what the hell is going on, because I doubt Nora came to visit this early in the morning wearing only a robe."

"I've been living here," Nora offered. "My house is being renovated, plus with morning sickness, and—"

"I asked her to move in."

"Why the hell would you do that?" Cruz demanded.

The brothers stared at each other a moment too long and the comfort level in the room plummeted.

"Is that because you're the father of her baby?" Cruz demanded.

The intense silence seemed to wrap them all in an uncomfortable blanket. Nora waited for one of the guys to speak. When the yawning quiet became too much, she swung her legs over the sofa and stood. She braced one hand on each of their shoulders, if for her support or to keep them from ripping each other apart, she didn't know.

"Cruz, we wanted to tell you," she started, her eyes on him. But he wasn't looking at her, only Zane.

"I told her to wait," Zane added. "I didn't want you to find out over the phone or when you were away on business."

The muscle in Cruz's jaw clenched and Nora was worried he'd haul off and punch his brother, but Cruz typically wasn't one to jump to anger or violence. He took a step back, then another, and his dark stare went from Zane to Nora.

"How long did you all sneak around before this?" he asked, his fists clenched at his sides. "Were you laughing behind my back or just didn't want to clue me in until you absolutely had to?"

"That's not how things went at all," Nora explained.

Zane held up his hand to stop her. "We weren't sneaking and we weren't laughing at you. Nothing happened between us until after you were gone, and it sure as hell wasn't planned."

Cruz stared between them for another moment before raking his hand over his jaw and letting out a bark of laughter. Nora had no idea what could possibly be funny right now, but she also had a hunch he wasn't feeling too humorous. There seemed to be a thread of sarcasm and frustration in that chuckle.

"This is not at all how I had this planned," he finally told them. "I never thought you two would work backward."

Confused, Nora glanced to Zane, whose attention still remained on his brother.

"What the hell are you talking about?" Zane demanded.

Nora reached for her mug, desperately needing the peppermint flavor. At this point, her tea had gone cold, but she didn't care. She welcomed anything that would help soothe the queasiness.

"I've wanted you two together for years," Cruz admitted. "You both danced around each other for so damn long, I took matters into my own hands. Clearly, you guys took off on your own before my plan fell into place."

"What plan?" Zane ground out.

Nora didn't know what the hell he was talking about and she had a sinking feeling this entire situation was about to get worse before it got better. Clearly, she and Zane weren't the only ones who had been keeping secrets. She didn't know why this irked the hell out of her, maybe it was the hormone overload, but she felt her blood pressure rising.

"The wedding shoot," Cruz confessed with a slight grin. "You two think you were hiding your emotions, but I know both of you better than you know yourselves. I figured if I could get Nora into a wedding gown and you overseeing the project in my absence, something might click."

"I don't want a marriage." Zane muttered a curse beneath his breath. "You know that."

Cruz shrugged. "You say you don't, but I also have seen how you look at Nora and how she looks at you."

What had she given away? More importantly, how had Cruz seen something from Zane when she never had?

"So you just thought you'd play matchmaker?" Zane said accusingly. "That's ridiculous."

"No, what's ridiculous is the two of you sneaking around."

"You're the one—"

"Stop!" Nora shouted. "Just stop arguing."

She set her tea back down, held out her hands, and glanced from one brother to the other. There were too many things going on at once, but if she had to find a bright side, at least the bomb from Cruz had taken her mind off her morning sickness.

"We all made mistakes," she started. "I think we're all sorry things happened the way they did, but none of us are trying to be hurtful. Right?"

The guys didn't say a word, so she took that as a yes. They continued to size each other up like fighting dogs, but she knew that anger wouldn't last. They had each other's backs and had been through it all.

"I have to say, I'm surprised you put so much thought into how to push us together," Nora admitted. "But I won't be manipulated into anything. Not a marriage, and not playing house and sharing a bed with a man who doesn't want me."

The more she thought about this entire scenario, the angrier she became. She faced Cruz fully and poked a finger at his chest. "Your plan didn't work. Your brother has no intention of ever marrying, not even to the woman who carries his child, and don't try to push me into a relationship again. I'm good."

Cruz opened his mouth to respond, but Nora turned and faced Zane. "And as for staying here until my renovations are over, I'm fine to return home. I've decided it's best to get back to my world and we can figure out this parenting thing without the sex coming into play."

"Nora, you're upset and not being logical."

"Oh, I'm definitely upset," she agreed. "I'd say we're all upset, but the longer I stay here, the more I'll want what you aren't willing to give. We both have demanding jobs and now a baby to concentrate on. That's more than enough."

When she started to turn away, Cruz slid his hand around her elbow. Nora glanced over her shoulder and met his dark stare.

"Zane is right," Cruz told her. "You should stay here until that work is done. Or if you don't want to stay here, then come to my place."

Nora eased from his grasp. "I think we all need our individual space right now, and my home is livable. It's just a mess. I'll make it work."

His lips thinned and there wasn't a doubt in her mind he wanted to argue. Nora turned back around and Zane had the same pained look on his face as well.

Too bad. They'd all made mistakes. Each one of them had every reason to be angry, but she wasn't kidding when she'd said they need to take time apart. There was too much hurt between them, and that's not the relationship she wanted with either guy. Despite being upset, she valued both of them and needed them in her life.

"I'm going to go pack my things."

As she started from the room, she wondered which brother would try to follow her and get her to stay. Nothing but silence followed her, and a piece of Nora crumbled. Maybe they had each damaged these relationships beyond repair, and maybe they would never get back to where they were before.

While she loved them both in totally different ways, she still had to look out for herself and her baby. Everything else had to fall in line behind them.

Sixteen

"Care to tell me what the hell is going on with the two of you?"

Zane crossed his ankle over his knee and stared across the living area to Barrett. Reluctantly, Zane and Cruz had come for that meeting Barrett had requested. They'd been there all of ten minutes and Zane was beyond ready to leave.

Nora had left his house four days ago and it might as well have been four months. The days seemed to drag and the damn house was too quiet. Even when he'd gone into the office, he'd pass by her door, which remained closed, and could practically feel the wedge between them.

Same with Cruz. He'd hardly spoken to his brother,

yet here they sat in Barrett's modest cottage on the edge of town.

"I understand you don't want to be here," Barrett told Zane, then he glanced at Cruz. "But what is up with you?"

"We're working through some things," Cruz admitted.

Barrett's narrowed eyes volleyed between Zane and his twin. Never before could Zane recall a time when he and his brother were at odds for this long. Oh, they bickered like any other set of siblings, but they never went days without talking. Not only could that destroy their personal relationship, but it could do heavy damage to *Opulence*.

"Tell me."

Zane shook his head. "We'll take care of it on our own time."

Barrett stood before them, propped his hands on his hips, and scoffed. "I might not have been around when you both needed me, but I'm here now. Let me help."

Zane didn't want his help. He didn't want to be here as well, but he couldn't stand to sit at his house in the silence, either. He'd gone with the lesser of the two evils.

"I'm not sure what you could do," Cruz stated, leaning forward on the sofa. "Zane and I both screwed up and managed to damage our relationship in addition to our relationships with Nora."

Barrett's thick brows drew in as he shook his head. "What does Nora have to do with this? Is there some love triangle or something?"

"No, hell no." Cruz raked his hands over his head and sighed. "I tried to fix them up because I thought they were perfect together, but—"

"Cruz."

Zane's sharp word cut off his brother's confession. Why the hell did they need to clue Barrett in on their business? They could keep everything private and work it out later.

"Let him finish," Barrett stated.

Zane glanced at his brother and Cruz simply shook his head.

"It's Zane's story to tell," he finally conceded. "I made a mistake, he made a mistake, and we've pissed each other off. That's all."

"And Nora is in the middle?"

Barrett took a seat in his recliner and eased back to start rocking. He tapped his hand on the arm as if contemplating his next thought or words.

"You're going to find out at some point," Zane found himself saying. "Nora is pregnant."

The chair stopped and Barrett's brows shot up toward his hairline. "So which one of you is the father?"

"Damn it, not me," Cruz exclaimed. "I've said we're just friends."

"There's a fine line between friends and something

more," Barrett explained. "I started out as friends with your mother and then you two came along."

Zane didn't say a word. What could he say? Letting his feelings fester seemed like the next logical step, right? He hadn't had a great relationship with his father in years, he and his brother were pissed at each other for justifiable reasons, and he had no clue where he stood with Nora. She'd moved out, but where did that leave them? Were they back to employee/boss and the friend zone? Just co-parenting? At some point, they would have to talk, but right now, Zane had to work on the relationships right here in this room.

"We need a drink." Barrett rocked upward and came to his feet. "No alcohol here, but how about some sweet tea or a soda?"

Zane shook his head no and Cruz asked for tea.

Barrett went to the small attached kitchen. Zane stared across the open space at his father and really studied the man as he busied himself playing the host.

His weathered hands, the creases around his eyes, the once-black hair now dotted with white. The years hadn't been kind to Barrett, but he hadn't lived the easiest life. All of his failures and setbacks had been brought on by his own actions. Instead of pulling himself up for his kids after his wife passed, he'd opted to be miserable and selfish, losing himself in the bottle and the world of gambling.

A sizable dose of guilt settled heavily in Zane's chest. Maybe he wasn't so far removed from being exactly like his father. No, Zane didn't have a spouse who had passed, but he'd had an amazing woman walk out of his life…and he'd just let her.

Even though Zane wasn't about to lose himself, there was that part of him that had a better understanding of how someone could self-destruct when their world fell apart. On the other hand, Zane couldn't imagine not being there for his child. He couldn't imagine just letting life pass him by.

Barrett came back and gave Cruz the tea, but he remained on his feet as he stared down at his sons.

"I'm sure neither of you want my advice, but I'm giving it anyway," he started. "I've learned my lesson that life is short and you have to find and create your own happiness. Waiting on someone else to turn your world around will never work. If you have any type of relationship with someone you care about, you'll put in the work to keep it, no matter the cost. I didn't put in the work with the two most important people in my life and I'm still paying for it."

Zane glanced at his twin, who was already looking back at him. They'd both messed up and had hurt each other, but they had a bond like no other.

"I really asked you guys to come here today just so I could see you," Barrett went on. "I didn't know you all had any turmoil going on, and I didn't know I was going to be a grandfather."

Zane jerked his attention back to Barrett.

"I mean, if you will allow that," he quickly added. "I know we're not on good terms, but the fact that you're here tells me you are willing to try to work on us."

Barrett stared for another minute, clutching his own tea and likely waiting on Zane to reply. The room settled in silence as Zane thought over the nugget of information he hadn't yet considered. Not once had he thought of Barrett as being a grandparent. But the look in the old man's eyes held something Zane hadn't seen in so long. Hope.

Maybe the baby he and Nora were expecting could tie them all together. Maybe this would be another layer of healing for all of them.

"I'll talk to Nora," Zane finally stated. "I can't make promises, but I'm not saying no."

Barrett's wide shoulders relaxed and a hint of a smile danced around his lips. "That's all I can ask for."

He took a seat back in his chair and set his tea on an old, worn coaster. "Now, what about the two of you?" he asked, gesturing a finger between them. "Can this be repaired?"

"Of course," Zane replied without thinking. "I'll admit I was wrong and he will, too."

"Will I?"

Zane glanced at his brother, who had a smirk on his face. "You know I hate being wrong," Cruz stated.

"Yeah, well, apologize and move on."

"I'm not apologizing."

Zane sighed. "Me, either."

"Perfect. We're even." Cruz gave a mock cheers gesture with his glass of tea and smiled. "All is right."

Zane knew it would be—at least between him and his twin. As for the relationship with Barrett, Zane had a kernel of faith that things were headed in the right direction. This relationship couldn't be patched up in one day or even one week, but one step at a time would add up. Maybe by the time Nora delivered, he and Barrett would be in a good place.

He just didn't know what place he and Nora would be in, and that entire situation lay directly on his shoulders.

For the past two weeks, Nora had lived through construction, and finally, the crew had left. Her home was all hers now, freshly painted and beautiful. Each room had some type of touch-up or complete overhaul. The deck out back added another level of living space she couldn't wait to enjoy this summer.

She stood in the empty nursery and envisioned a crib and a rocker, a changing table and white shelves full of cardboard books.

Maybe she was still early in her pregnancy, but she wanted everything done and ready for when her baby arrived. Well, the room would be ready—she wasn't so sure about her relationship with Zane.

She hadn't spoken to him or Cruz since she left

his house. At some point, she'd reach out, but she was still struggling with all the deceit that had surrounded them.

Her doorbell chimed through her house and Nora stilled. She only knew two people who would show up unannounced. Pulling in a deep breath, she headed down the hall toward her entryway. She glanced down at her clothes and figured her appearance didn't matter. She'd come home from work and put on the most comfortable thing she owned: her old hoodie from college and a pair of leggings.

Nora reached the door and stood on her tiptoes to see out the top window. Then she flicked the lock and opened the door to her uninvited guest.

"Why are you ringing the doorbell?" she asked. "You've never done that since we've known each other."

Cruz slid his hands into the pockets of his jeans and shrugged. "I wasn't sure if you'd care that I used my key, and I wasn't taking any chances that I'd actually be welcome."

He offered her that sheepish grin she'd seen so many times from him...the same grin Zane had worn when he'd given her that box with teas and a new mug.

"Of course you're welcome." She stepped aside for him to enter. "You're my first visitor since the reno project. The crew actually finished up this morning."

Cruz glanced around and made his way through

the living area and kitchen. As he passed the new wall of glass doors leading to the new patio, he did a double take.

"This looks awesome, Nora."

Flipping the switch by the door, he turned the exterior lights on, then opened the sliding doors until the entire wall vanished. The crew had put in a sunken firepit with seating all around. A swaying swing hung suspended from the porch's rafters, and a table long enough to feed a small army ran the length of the space. All money well spent.

"They did a remarkable job," he stated again, then turned to face her as she stepped out to join him. "But I didn't come to discuss your renovations."

Nora fisted her hands inside her hoodie. "No, I'm sure you didn't. Why don't you take a seat?"

Cruz went to the swing and sat, then patted the seat beside him for her to join. Nora couldn't deny him. He'd been her very best friend for far too long. Besides, she'd kept a secret from him, so they were on an even field. But she still wasn't happy about being duped.

"Are you feeling okay?" he asked as he eased the swing into a gentle motion.

"I'm good. Glad to be back home."

"Are you really?"

Nora's stomach was tied in knots, and she couldn't lie. There had been more than enough of that going around.

"Honestly, no. I'm not." She shifted until her back was against the cushioned arm of the swing and her legs were stretched out on his lap. "Your brother is infuriating."

Cruz laughed as he rested his hands on her legs. "He can be."

Nora tried to find the right way to explain her frustrations, but first, she had to clear the air.

"I'm sorry we didn't tell you about us," she began. "Well, not that there's an *us*, but you know what I mean. We just didn't think we should say anything while you were gone and we were trying to be private about everything."

Cruz tipped his head her way. "You think you and my brother aren't one unit? I assure you, you are."

"I wouldn't be back home if we were."

Alone in her bed, alone in her thoughts. She didn't realize how much she'd gotten used to a warm body by her side and someone to fall asleep chatting with each night. How could she have gotten so accustomed to the man after such a short time?

"He's confused," Cruz explained. "Probably afraid to admit how he really feels."

"I'm not sure if he's afraid or if he just doesn't feel." That was the hardest part to try to understand and likely accept. "There's a good chance he got what he wanted from me and he's just done."

"Don't say that," Cruz scolded. "You know Zane doesn't use anyone, let alone women."

She rested her head against the back of the swing and knew the truth in her heart.

"He never has before, that I'm aware of." She toyed with the frayed end of one of the strings from her hood. "But what else am I supposed to think? Aside from having a child together, we really connected on a deeper level. I thought he had stronger feelings for me. Clearly, I was foolish for putting myself in this position."

Cruz eased toward her, his hand resting on her knee. The glow from the new exterior lights gave her a perfect view of the compassion staring back at her.

"I don't want your pity," she scolded. "Can we pretend Zane isn't your brother and you're just my friend giving me advice like always?"

He gave her knee a gentle squeeze. "We can pretend anything you want, but the truth is that right now Zane is torn between what he wants and what he thinks he wants."

"That doesn't make sense," she retorted.

"He wants you—that much is obvious. But he's programmed himself to think that he doesn't need anyone."

"I'm positive he doesn't need me or he would've fought for me to stay."

"We were at our dad's house the other night," Cruz informed her, then blew out a heavy breath. "I didn't know what would happen, but I'm pretty sure Dad and Zane are on a path to something better."

Nora dropped her string and rested her hand on Cruz's. "That's great for all of you. What happened to make Zane go there and turn a new leaf?"

"You."

Surprised, Nora jerked slightly. "Me? I didn't do anything other than listen to him talk about your childhood. I gave him some advice, but you know how stubborn he is."

"This baby and your love have changed him," Cruz insisted. "He's not the same man he was when I left."

Nora snorted. "He doesn't love me. Trust me on that one."

"What makes you say that? Because he seems pretty damn protective of you. He's never had a woman live with him before."

"I wasn't living there." Nora pulled her hand away and snuggled it back into the pouch of her hoodie. "My house was torn up and I had morning sickness."

"Is that why you were in only a robe and he was in a pair of shorts when I came by the other day? Because that wasn't just Zane being kind."

Okay, so they had been much more than temporary roommates.

"Regardless, he's made it clear from the start that we aren't going to be more than what we are now. He refuses to open up and let love in."

"Why are you giving him the option?" Cruz demanded. "The Nora I know takes charge of what she wants."

"I told him how I feel. The information is his to do what he wants with it." Her heart still hurt, because that confession had been two weeks ago. "His silence speaks volumes."

"What did he say when he saw you in those wedding dresses?"

Nora popped her head up and narrowed her eyes. "That was pretty damn sneaky of you."

A wide smile spread across his face. The man had no remorse about his little stunt.

"You're not even sorry, are you?"

"Not at all," he admitted. "I bet Zane had no clue what to say when you came out. And I refuse to have regrets, because I saw a couple of the rough shots and I don't know how anyone could edit those to make you look better. You were stunning, Nora. I knew you would be, so there was a method to my madness."

"Oh, you were mad all right. I'm not a model, Cruz, but you all had your fun. I'm retiring."

He chuckled and patted her as he started the swing in motion once again.

"You're a model—you just don't want to be," he retorted. "Sort of like Zane being in love with you when he just doesn't want to be. You're both afraid. But I'm an outsider looking in and I'm telling you that you two are perfect together."

Yeah, well, Zane wasn't having any part of that, so Cruz would just have to meddle in someone else's life.

"Let's forget about me for a bit," Nora suggested. "How did the model search go?"

Cruz groaned and rubbed his forehead.

"That good, huh?"

"Oh, it went fine, but Mila is going to be a handful."

Her mind raced through the prospects he'd gone to meet with.

"Mila," Nora murmured. "Oh, is she the one from the Dominican Republic?"

"No. She's from Miami, and I don't know if her attitude or her hair is bigger. She'll be here next month for a trial shoot. We'll see if her ego and mine can get along."

Nora couldn't help but laugh, because Cruz could get along with anyone, so she wondered how this Mila would work out.

She reached out and slid her hand over his arm. "I missed you."

"Yeah, I missed you, too. Now, do you want my help with Zane?"

"Oh, no. You've done enough, and he knows where I stand. The rest is up to him."

Cruz simply stared at her and she could see his wheels in motion. But anything beyond this point was up to Zane. She wasn't begging and she wasn't about to let Cruz play mediator.

Part of her hoped her best friend was right. She hoped Zane did love her and would have enough courage to admit it.

But it was his other words that really hit her hard. She did always go after what she wanted and never let fear stand in her way. So now she had a choice to make.

Wait and see. Or take action.

Seventeen

"Sir. A delivery."

Zane glanced up from his phone, where he'd pulled up Nora's number for at least the twentieth time over the past few days. He didn't know what to say and knew a text wasn't the way to go, but he hated staying silent.

Yet without the proper words, that's exactly what he'd done.

"Just bring it in and set it over there." Zane motioned for his assistant, Will, to put the package on the table near the door. "I'll get to it later."

He typed out the one thing he needed her to know, but didn't hit Send. How could he deliver this over a text message? That wouldn't do at all. He had to see her. He had to fight for what he wanted, no matter the risk or the chances of getting hurt.

"It's rather large," Will added, still in the doorway.

Confused, Zane slid his phone aside and stood. He shouldn't have an order, but that didn't mean anything. Being the CEOs, both he and Cruz would get special deliveries on occasion, often from social media gurus who wanted to capture their attention.

Intrigued, he crossed the office just as his assistant wheeled in a giant image. The canvas stood taller than him and had to be six feet wide. The purple cloth draped over the entire image shielded what it could be.

"I can take it from here, Will. Thank you."

Nora breezed around from the other side of the oversize delivery. She braced her hands on the edge and wheeled it out of the way before offering Will a smile. The young man's brows drew in as he tried to see what was going on, but Nora closed the door before turning to face Zane.

His breath caught in his throat. She looked too damn good, and he hadn't seen her for weeks. Every part of him had wanted to tell her to come back, but what then? What if she came back and he couldn't be the man she wanted…the man she deserved?

She'd put on another one of her fitted, yet classy, dresses, this one in a bold red. Her hair lay as smooth as silk over one shoulder, and she wore a simple pair of nude heels. The woman looked every bit the part of a business exec, but he wanted to know what she wore beneath that dress and if there was any chance in hell he'd ever find out.

"You look good." The words came out before he could think, but he wasn't sorry. "Are you feeling better in the mornings?"

"I'm perfectly fine."

She didn't even look his way as she gave the cloth a yank and revealed the image.

Zane blinked, unable to believe what he was seeing.

"You seemed to love these shots so much, so I chose my favorite for you to keep in here," she explained, as if going over some business plan. "I know I balked at modeling for this, but you were right. I do look great, and we look perfect together."

His eyes ran over the blown-up photo. The pose with her head resting on his shoulder as she smiled sweetly for the camera...

Zane remained still as his throat filled with emotions. He remembered that exact moment with her, but he hadn't seen this shot and hadn't seen the expression on her face...until now.

"You were right about something else, too," she went on.

Now he turned his attention to her as she took a step toward him. Zane remained by his desk, unable to move or even think. He had to concentrate on her words and how perfect she looked in person and in that photo, which seemed to be mocking him.

"I do deserve better than what you were giving me."

Her words penetrated that hazy fog in his mind. He knew she'd come to this conclusion, but he didn't know how he'd feel about it. Right now, a good bit of fear held him captive, but not fear of his emotions. No. This fear stemmed from losing her.

"I deserve someone who will put me first," she went on, ticking off her fingers. "Put our relationship first. I need someone who will take me and my child, because we are a package deal."

Rage bubbled in him. Like hell would any man raise his child or sleep next to his woman. He refused to believe he was too late. He wouldn't let Nora slip out of his life simply because he'd been too damn afraid to face what was right in front of him.

She had to know the truth. The time had come for him to face his emotions and say them out loud. If he'd learned nothing else from her, he'd learned to be bold and take chances.

"Nora—"

Her sharp gaze cut to him. "I'm not done."

Growing more and more frustrated, Zane crossed his arms and widened his stance as he waited for her to finish. He had a few words to say himself.

"If we're going to co-parent, you're going to have to accept whoever I bring into my life, because you had your chance and—"

In a flash, Zane snaked his arms around her waist. He caught Nora's gasp with his mouth as he kissed her to shut up the nonsense she'd been spewing.

Her body melted against his as she clutched his shoulders. Finally, he had her back in his arms, where she belonged. She opened her mouth beneath his, sweeping her tongue with as much passion as always.

Zane settled his hands on her waist and eased back just enough to catch his breath.

"Did my plan work?" she asked.

"Plan?"

Nora pushed back and that wide smile on her face hit him right in the gut. She was so damn beautiful and everything he thought he didn't need. How could he have been so foolish to ever think he could live without her?

"You think I was just going to let you walk away and live in misery?" she asked. "I know you're scared of love, but ignoring it won't make it go away."

Zane slid his hands to her back and tugged her again to where he wanted her against his chest. "No kidding. I've been miserable and my house is too damn quiet. Everywhere I look, I see empty walls and find myself wondering what color you'd paint them or where you would put all of those pictures you love. I need you there or we can build somewhere else or, hell, move into your place. I don't care, but I'm not spending another night without you."

Nora's eyes closed as she released a breath. "I'm so glad you said that, because I contacted a Realtor this morning to put my house up for sale."

"What?"

She blinked and refocused on him. "We're raising our family in your house and we're having family get-togethers, and we're going to let your father into our lives and give him that chance he deserves. I want it all and I want it with you. I'd even let you paint our bedroom white."

Zane kissed her once again as his heart swelled with all the emotions. His future, *their* future as a family, seemed to have endless possibilities.

"I'm not taking no for an answer on any of this, by the way," she added.

"I wouldn't dream of telling you no." He glanced toward the intrusive canvas. "Where is that really going? Or do I even want to know?"

She laughed and patted his cheek. "In our house."

Our house. Damn, but he did love the sound of that.

"You know, I was going to come to you," he admitted. "I couldn't find the right words to say."

She quirked one perfectly arched brow. "Is that right?"

Zane released her and went to grab his cell from his desk. The screen was still pulled up from the text he'd never sent. He handed the device over and watched for her expression.

"That's all the words I had."

Her eyes filled as she glanced from the phone up to him.

"I couldn't send it, because that's something that needs to be said in person," he went on.

Zane took the cell from her hands and slid it into his pocket before reaching for her once again. He curled one hand around her waist and cupped her cheek with the other. With the pad of his thumb, he swiped away the single tear that had trickled down.

"I do love you," he confessed. "I didn't realize how freeing that would be to admit, but nothing has ever felt more perfect or right."

She sniffed and let out a watery laugh, throwing her arms around his neck.

"I love you, and I've been waiting on you to say those words to me. I can't believe this is happening." She tipped her head back and dropped kisses all over his face. "I can't wait to tell Cruz."

"Oh, hell," Zane groaned. "He'll think his plan worked and he played matchmaker."

Nora held his face in her hands. "Let him think what he wants. I don't care how we got together, we are now and that's all that matters. But there's one more thing."

"What's that?" he asked.

"Can we get a dog? I'm really missing Clara, and you have the perfect yard for one to run free and—"

He cut her off with a kiss. Spinning her around so he could reach behind her and lock his office door. When he released her, she had a wide smile across her face.

"We can get any dog you want, but I am drawing the line at that ostrich," he told her.

Nora rolled her eyes. "Fine, but if one shows up at our wedding reception, just go with it."

Go with it. He had a feeling that would be the motto for their marriage and he couldn't wait to make it official.

* * * * *

Look for the next story in this duet!

One Stormy Night

Available April 2023!

HARLEQUIN
PLUS

Try the best multimedia subscription service for romance readers like you!

Read, Watch and Play.

Experience the easiest way to get the romance content you crave.

Start your **FREE TRIAL** at
www.harlequinplus.com/freetrial.